Six Neckties

Johnny Diaz

Published by
Johnny Diaz
On Amazon CreateSpace

Six Neckties
ISBN: 1537183419
ISBN 13: 9781537183411

Acknowledgments

THIS BOOK IS dedicated to Yato and Luna for adding love, support and (lots of dog hair) to my life. I'd like to thank my wonderful god-mother Maria Sanchez and the Sanchez/Ferullo/Henry clan for always reading my work. I'd also like to thank my tios Aldo and Maria Cuervo for their unconditional love. And a big thanks to my loyal readers especially Tony and Terrence who have stuck by me ever since I first published Boston Boys Club.

1

HERE WE GO again! I know the cues by heart. They begin with the harpist as she gently serenades the guests with each pluck of the chords. That cues the groom's mother and father as they escort him down the aisle while his husband-to-be awaits. The groom being walked down the aisle this afternoon is my friend Rico, my wingman for the past 10 years. I'm back at the altar supporting him but I'm not the one getting married. This is his wedding to Oliver, his boyfriend for the past two years.

As Rico and his parents slowly stride to the altar, I make a mental checklist of my best man duties. Black tuxedo, check. Ring in hand, check. Necktie perfectly positioned, check.

This has been my recurring role over the years since same-sex marriage became legal in New England states and other parts of the country. And it all started with Massachusetts, my former home state which redefined gay love legally and culturally. Other states followed, presenting more gay men and lesbians with an option they hadn't really considered before. Engagements, bachelor and bache-lorette parties, bridal showers, weddings and yes divorces but I think of myself as a romantic optimist so let's focus on the weddings like the one I'm attending this afternoon.

Over the years, the invitations to participate in my friends' nuptials have gotten annoyingly more frequent. When you have close guy friends both gay and straight from the Bay State to the Sunshine State who have a propensity for finding that special person and falling in love – with you know, *the* one - you're the buddy they turn to for best man duties, to pen a poem for the occasion or raise a toast.

I've got each one down pact!

I always say yes because at the end of the day, I know that I helped someone I love and care about enjoy the most important day of their life. Hence, my various neckties - four to be exact- including the bright pink one that I'm sporting now. The official wedding colors are charcoal grey and blush pink. Don't ask. It was Rico's mother's idea. Speaking of, mine is a little tight under the collar so I fidget with it as I watch Rico tightly grin at all the guests on both sides of the aisle. Oh, the sacrifices you make for your buds. I know that when true love finds its way home to me again, my friends will be there as I have been for them. Call it good wedding karma.

But I digress. Today isn't about me. This is Rico and Oliver's special day and Rico right now looks nervous. He keeps dabbing sweat off his forehead with his pink handkerchief. I raise my eyebrows and look at him bug-eyed to lighten the mood. I then silently mouth, "You're doing great, amigo!" and wiggle my thick black eyebrows like Charlie Chaplin. He quickly sticks out his tongue at me and he continues dabbing his forehead. When they finally reach the steps to the altar, Rico's parents hug and kiss him and hand him over to Oliver whose hazel eyes begin to mist at the sight of his future husband standing before him. How did Rico get here first? I've always been more the wide-eyed romantic while he was well, let me explain. Some background notes on our best friend-ship.

Rico has been my best friend, my Italian –American brother from another mother since I first moved to Boston. I was a youngish lad then, in my late 20s to be exact. I reverse-migrated to Irish-Boston from Hispanic-Miami and we instantly became each other's bro. He was the tough-talking accountant with green eyes that matched the color of his Italian tattoo on his bulging right bicep. I was the curly-haired slight Cuban-American trying to make it as a journalist in Boston. Rico always had a wall around his heart from failed romances with the wrong guys. They were really trysts with the guys falling for Rico but he never reciprocated because my friend was about beers and boys. I wore my heart on my sleeve, looking for Mr. Right who I thought I had found in Mikey but that relationship spilled into a big mess like a glass of vodka and diet Coke at Club Café (my drink of choice which I could use a double right about now, in this setting.)

And while my romance went up in smoke twice because I apparently didn't learn my lesson from the first time around with Mikey, Rico managed to land his own Mr. Right. With his kind soul, piercing eyes, crew cut and warm heart, Oliver hooked Rico for good. Oliver wasn't a trick that Rico could simply leave behind. Rico fell in love with his caring nature, his masculine tenderness and his ability to look at the good in everything including Rico. Before I forget to mention, Oliver is a research scientist at a Boston drug company so he's hella smart too. I know he'll take good care of my old friend. If not, I'll do some Cuban voodoo on him. (I picked up some habits over the years from my late mother.)

But I don't think Oliver will break Rico's heart. They're in this for the long haul. Besides, their sex is akin to the Fourth of July fireworks display over the Esplanade along the Charles River. At least that's how Rico has described it to me. When Rico and I are together, we're like two frat brothers who never grew up. We laugh, exchange stories and drinks. And I can't wait to rib him over how he's turning into a mushy puddle of tears right now at his own wedding. I can't really blame him. How often do we gay men get the chance to marry?

Back to the wedding, Oliver gently takes Rico hands as they stand before Reverend Faith Wilkinson who welcomes everyone to the ceremony.

"We are gathered here today to celebrate the union of Oliver Doyle and Rico DiMio...." she begins with a soft soothing voice. Rico looks up at Oliver, who stands six-feet-two to Rico's five-foot-nine frame (same as mine) and radiates pure love toward his groom.

I look down at the beige carpeting of this reception hall which faces the cold dark blue waters of Provincetown on this Friday in June. I glance farther behind the grand windows behind the altar as sunlight pours in, lighting up this hall with a celestial glow. It's a perfect day for a wedding and this little gay tourist town at the tip of the state has become a draw for couples all over the US looking to tie the knot.

I can't wait for my own special day. Like my fellow gay brothers and sisters, I had never considered marriage before. Growing up in a traditional Cuban Catholic home in Miami Beach, gay men weren't supposed to exchange vows under the Father, the Son and the Holy Spirit. Society said so, for uh...ever since the Catholic Church started 2,000 years ago. So I put the thought out of my mind whenever I attended a cousin's wedding in Miami or when my parents, Pepe and Gladys, marked their anniversary each July with my father surprising my mom with a bouquet of roses. It was the same gift every year yet my mom acted like it was the best gift ever. That's true love. They posed by the grand fake-gold rimmed mirror in our living room, swapped champagne glasses and kisses. If I was home from Boston at the time, I captured the moment and added it to their years of anniversary photos. Same setting, same pose, just a different year but the same powerful true love. *Ahh, love!*

It's not that Cupid hasn't shot me with his arrow. It just shot the wrong guy whom I thought was *the* one. I've been in love and fell hard, twice to one guy. That's Mikey, a blue-eyed younger Ethan Hawke clone but with better teeth.

Mikey.

Where should I begin? The first time we dated was for six months during my first year in Boston. He was an active alcoholic, seduced by the tall statuesque figure of a Corona bottle. His hangovers, reckless driving and sloppy bar visits (which always ended with me carrying him out of Club Café and taking him to my studio apartment in Harvard Square) served as a quick education in alcoholism. No matter how hard I tried to get him to get some help, he preferred the Corona over me. We parted ways. I walked away but my heart still pined for Mikey. No more "Hey cutie!" whenever he called or texted me.

A few months later, he sobered up and sought me out as a friend. I chose to give him a second chance, as a friend. Our relationship reignited like a match. The love had never gone away. We picked up where we left off with our weekend trips to Providence and Maine and late night cuddle-a-thons while watching romantic comedies and Marvel super hero movies on the sofa. But my emotional scars from our first trip down romance lane lingered like a dark cloud that shadowed me. And even though he had sought help and sobered up, there were some issues he needed to work out on his own. So I broke it off seeking someone more stable. I also broke his heart and mine because I still haven't met anyone who understood me so well, who could make me smile or laugh with a certain look. We were each other's yin to yang physically, mentally (he was a school teacher) and emotionally (he always left me sweet notes hidden in my apartment.) No matter what we did (from losing my Jeep at Providence Place mall to getting lost in Dorchester at night or running from a swarm of flies in the Blue Hills during a weekend hike), we had fun in our adventures. We were best friends and passionate lovers. We shared a sweet intimacy, one that our friends and family observed and understood. Most of all, Mikey saw me, the real me for good and bad (the latter mostly me being OCD and stuck to my routines of wanting to eat at Boston Market and drinking Diet Coke all the time.) I've had dates here and there since then but no luck. I identify as 100 percent single. I'm married to the single life. But enough with my gay version of a bad country love song, I should be focused on Rico's nuptials.

"The ring, Tommy, the ring!" the reverend repeats which snaps me out of my train of thought.

I sheepishly smile as I quickly pull out the wedding band from the right pocket of my blazer.

"Sorry!" I squeak, handing it over.

Rico lifts his right eyebrow and then smirks at me.

"Sorry," I silently mouth and awkwardly smile.

We're almost done with the ceremony. Here comes my favorite part when the couple dreamily stares into each other's eyes and seals the deal.

"Will you Rico, take this man Oliver to be your loving husband for sickness and poorer until death to you part?" the reverend asks.

"I will," Rico says, tears pooling in his eyes as he slides a ring on Oliver's finger.

"And do you Oliver take this man to be your lawfully wedded husband, to have and to hold, for this day forward..."

"I will," Oliver says smiling, a dimple in each cheek. I groove in place and smile proudly from my front-row perch to all the action (one of the benefits of being a best man.) You are *right there* and we're almost there.

Oliver then places his ring on Rico's finger.

They hold hands and lean forward.

"By the power vested in me, I now pronounce you husband and husband!"

My smile widens to its physical limits. Rico and Oliver exchange a sweet long wet kiss. The harpist begins to play again and the hall breaks out in a chorus of loud cheering applause. I hear an occasional "Whoo hoo" and "MOLTO BENE RICARDO" from the crowd of guys from Rico's Italian side of the family.

Rico and Oliver pull back from their kiss and hold their hands high in triumph. They made it! Their faces wreathed in smiles.

I clap so hard that my hands turn red. I'm just feeling so proud and happy for my amigo. They begin their walk back up the aisle as all the fellow groomsmen -starting with me - begin the same walk out of the hall and then outside for photos. And another wedding bites the dust. Necktie #4!

Before I continue any further, let me introduce myself. Some of you may be familiar with my name or at least my byline. I'm Tommy Perez, a former *Boston Daily* newspaper features reporter and current *People* magazine staff writer. Like my name suggests, I'm Cuban and American, a rare combination where I live now, in uber-white Ogunquit Maine.

Because I am a roving reporter based in New England, I parachute from story to story which ironically sometimes include the big celebrity weddings. (Who do you think gathers all the colorful details such as the who's-who in attendance, who wore what, the exact number of flowers and what was served at the reception?) Every few days, I report from a different city but I get to work from apartment. My bedroom is also my writer's cove/office and the view can be distracting. Sometimes my mind drifts off as I study the cliff walk off Marginal Way where the Atlantic beach breezes blow in and the sounds of sea gulls caw in the distance. This is why I chose to relocate here from Dorchester – the solitude and serenity this small town provides me when I work. I also wanted to stop bumping into Mikey on my nights out in Boston.

In the last few weeks, I've covered the filming of a new movie starring a certain Boston actor who used to rap in his undies. The movie is still being shot in South Boston. That story was followed by one about *The Real House Maids of Providence*, Rhode Island and the start of their new season. The Encore channel's Randy Zohan invited the magazine (that's me) for an exclusive behind-the-scenes look of the new season for a future issue of the magazine.

I also covered a Make-A-Dream-Come True request of a nine-year-old boy in Vermont who wanted to be a super hero for the day. That story touched my heart because Jimmy suffers from a rare case of leukemia. To make his dream come true, firefighters and police

officers coordinated a day of rescue situations including a missing
dog so that Jimmy could sport a blue and yellow cape and boots to
save the day. Hey, not all of our stories are celebrity-based. Once in a
while, we get the average person in our magazine. It is called *People,*
people.

And I also recently covered the wedding of a major Latina TV
star who's a regular on one of the hottest sitcoms on network televi-
sion. She married the magazine's pick for hottest bachelor from last
year so we had to cover the event and give it the cover story treat-
ment. That wedding took place in the green rolling mountains of the
Berkshires in Massachusetts.

So weddings seem to be a regular theme in my life and yet I feel
like I'm destined to be perpetually single. I don't know why. It's as if
Cupid rescinded his love arrow from my heart and put it on layaway
until I have proven myself love worthy again after I dumped Mikey
during our second attempt at a healthy and stable relationship. I did
my best to deal with his alcoholism and recovery but whenever a situation arose like the time he lied to me about not wanting to meet up
with one of my close friends Carlos Martin or when he confessed to
having snuck in a few drinks at one of my work parties, the mental
and emotional exhaustion returned like a rolling noreaster' off the
Maine coast. Not again, I thought. My heart and patience just petered
out and I wanted out, for good. Still, I kinda miss him.

So basically everything that you might see on *Entertainment
Tonight* on any given night, I cover but through a New England lens.
On my downtime, I run along Ogunquit Beach where the ocean's steel-
blue chilly water stings (and sometimes freezes) my feet. Or I may
drive to New Hampshire and hike 3,000 feet up Mount Monadnock
and take in the sweeping views of the hiking trails and forests which
together look like a giant green comforter blanketing the region. I'll
walk along the historic red bricked-buildings by the wharf of downtown Portland and marvel at the boats and cruise ships that dock
there. And sometimes, I drive down to Boston to visit Rico and Carlos,

my fellow Beantown Cuban who is also about to be married in a few weeks. (Another necktie to add to my collection!)

That's the beauty of New England, you can hop in your car (in my case, that's an orange Volkswagen Beetle) and head to another state within an hour. Compare that to Miami where you have to drive eight hours north to cross the Florida-Georgia line.

Still, despite my successful career as a magazine writer and my good guy friends, I find myself 'liking' photos of couples on Facebook and Instagram. I fantasize what it may be like to have that special person by my side again. I've had the occasional date and hookup (I'm still a horny Latino at heart) but the dates and the hookups for that matter don't seem to go anywhere. Like a Snapchat message, they come and go. Ever since Grindr, Scruff and other alleged dating apps have appeared on the scene, guys seem to have forgotten what a traditional date looks like. You know (or maybe not), a dinner, drinks, a movie, a romantic stroll along the bay, a long deep kiss good night at the door. A nice Hallmark card saying how great the night was. Okay, maybe I am pushing it there but a guy can fantasize, right?

Speaking of dates to remember, Rico and Oliver are smooching during the photo shoot on the dock behind the hall. They lean into each other as the photographer, a cute, lean, blue-eyed guy, snaps away. He positions them in front of the grand white hall of the facility for some photos. Then he directs them to a white bench for some sit-down pictures with Provincetown's harbor in the background.

"Now hold your hands in this one guys. Yeah, perfect!" the photographer instructs. "Keep it right there. Beautiful!" Rico and Oliver rest their heads against one another's, look down and smile. They look so handsome like poster boys for gay marriage.

"HEY, BEST MAN! TOMMY PEREZ! Come over here," the photographer barks at me. Although he's cute in that Ben Feldman way but taller, I'm annoyed by the sudden command. He waves his hand and roughly positions me between Rico and Oliver. A manwich.

"Very handsome guys," the photographer says.

"Thanks but what's your name again? I don't think I caught it the first time," I say, changing poses with Rico for the various takes.

"I'm Danny!" he says from behind the black bulky camera.

"And that's the perfect shot. Thanks BEST MAN! Can I get all the groomsmen for a group photo! NOW!" Danny shouts. The rest of the guys scramble in position like penguins in grey suits with pink ties and matching handkerchief squares in their front pockets.

"Yo, BEST MAN, you need to be next to this groom," Danny says. Ugh. He's a bit bossy. This is a wedding after all. Can't he be a little nicer? This isn't boot camp.

"YES SIR!" I respond like a private in the army. I hold my hand over the rim of my eyebrows, march in place and salute. That makes Danny grin.

Rico then whispers into my ear, "I never thought you liked the drill sergeant type. This guy likes to give orders."

"Um, he needs to work on his delivery. Where did you find this guy?" I say to Rico from the side of my mouth as Danny snaps some photos.

"Hey guys, no talking. SMILE PLEASE!"

"OKAY!" everyone shouts back in a gaggle of giggles, showing off their pearly whites. Danny immediately pops some shots.

"He's a friend of the family. He came highly recommended. Oliver and I saw his work. You should see his photos, among other things."

"Oh no, is he one of your old hookups?" I whisper to Rico who glares at me.

"No silly goose! I never messed with guys who knew my parents or grandparents. That could be fucking sticky. I knew him from grow-ing up. He was always at our family events. Nice guy even if he's being a bit loud right now."

"Focus guys! One, two…and we got the shot! Good job everybody. Now, where are the grooms' parents?" Danny says loudly. "Come on, let's go. We're on a tight schedule."

The groomsmen all shuffle away and head to the open outside bar on the dock as Rico's parents and Oliver's parents get in position for the photos. I order my usual vodka and Diet Coke from the slight bartender with a crew cut. I tip him $5 just because I think he's cute in a Jonas brother kind of way (The younger two not the chubby married one.) Soft festive music plays in the background as the guests mill about with their glasses of champagne and cocktails.

As soon as I have my drink in hand, I marvel at Rico and Oliver celebrating their moment. But I also can't help notice how attractive Danny is with his wavy black hair, big blue eyes and chiseled jawline. Although he's loud and a little obnoxious with his orders, he seems to be doing a good job, capturing Rico and Oliver in different poses from standing shoulder-to-shoulder to Rico sitting on Oliver's lap with his arm around him. In between the takes, Rico looks my way and I wink, nod and hold up my glass. He crosses his eyes, makes a silly face and sticks out his tongue again. I'm so happy to be a part of a friend's wedding once again.

"Yo BEST MAN! Stop distracting the groom!" Danny shouts my way with an annoyed smirk. I give him my best withering stare and hold up my glass toward him. And I wonder, who is this guy and where did he come from?

2

I'M SMILING AS my index finger grazes across each of Rico and Oliver's wedding photos on my iPad. In one photo, they stand shoulder to shoulder and laugh on the dock in their sleek grey suits and matching pink ties. Another image captures their silhouette as they lean in for a kiss. And another image shows them smearing vanilla cake all over each other's mouths. What a beautiful day! I can't believe that was a week ago and the guys are still on their honeymoon in Italy where they are exploring Rico's ancestry.

When I reach the end of the photo gallery, there's a signature stamp that reads, *Photos by Danny DiNozzio* with his contact information. There's a small photo of Danny holding up a camera which covers half his face. Using my index finger and thumb, I expand the image and get a better look at Danny and his tuft of dark hair and twinkling blue eyes. And I wonder, is he single? But wait, what am I doing?

From what I remember, Rico said the guy travels a lot and is based in western Massachusetts where Rico's family lives. We didn't seem to get along with all his barking orders. But there's something in his photos that strikes me and grabs my attention, stirring something within me. Despite his gruff demeanor, Danny trained his lens to capture the magical connection between my friend and his groom.

It's those intimate moments that some photographers instinctively know how to find frame by frame, a skill you can't learn in a classroom or from using a selfie stick. Like an artist or a dancer, you've either got it or you don't. You're born with it and Danny definitely has the photo gene. I relaunch the photo gallery and scan the photos and admire Danny's prowess behind the camera. He not only captured the grooms in small intimate moments but also their family members and friends (me of course) bantering and unaware that he was nearby shooting. Actually, I'm in several of the photos grinning or nodding my head back, lost in the humor of a conversation with a guest. And more importantly, Danny captured my good side (which is my right.) But once again, I digress. The guy knew what was he doing. I wonder what other jobs he has lined up? What other photography work he's done? And how big is his lens, so to speak? I catch myself grinning at the former.

These thoughts swim through my head as I sit inside a coffee shop along the main highway in Ogunquit. A clog of cars flows through the town. Throngs of families shuffle by on their way to the many small art galleries and mom-and-pop cafes on this golden and cool June afternoon. There's just enough of a breeze rolling off the ocean that it soothes the skin and cleanses the soul. That's one of the reasons I defected north – the beach healing. No matter how stressed out I am over my magazine assignments, I just walk down a block or two to the beach and just be. Perhaps it's all in my head but I feel good when I'm near the water. I credit that to the healing properties of the beach breezes, the never-ending blue horizon and the sounds of the rushing waves.

As I Zen myself out, I also notice gay couples, mostly men, walking, talking and laughing as they sip their drinks or munch on a cookie or cupcake from one of the local bakeries. I lean back in my wooden chair, sip my iced tea as the sun pours through the front glass windows and warms my face. The afternoon light illuminates the weathered wooden floors and tables, making the coffee shop look more like a library but with plush sofas and empty coffee cups.

With Rico hitched and away on vacation, I'm feeling more unattached than ever but that has been my life in Ogunquit and I've embraced it. I work. I read. I write. I sleep. I bop around town and nearby Kittery and Portland in my Volkswagen which looks like an orange jelly bean with four wheels. And I take long, well short walks to nowhere in this artsy town. I also make time to text or call my friends in other New England states such as Carlos in Cambridge.

To help chase away the recent bout of single's blues, I reached out to him when I arrived at the coffee house about an hour ago. I asked him if we could hang in Boston this afternoon. Being with Carlos always felt like home, a mix of Boston and Miami. We can drop words in Spanish, gab about our families and gossip about which guys we think are hot in Boston even though Carlos has been with Nick for two years.

"Oye, of course! Come on down! We can go to our old hang out, the Border Café and catch up. I haven't been there as much since you moved to Canada, I mean Maine. I want to hear all about Rico's wedding so bring your iPad so I can check out the photos. It may give me some ideas for my day with Nick in Key West," Carlos said, his voice filled with excitement earlier today.

"You're still going to write a speech for the wedding, right, loco? I can't think of anyone else who knows me as well as you do and who can find the right mix of English and Spanish for our guests!"

"Of course! You're like my Cuban brother. Rico is my Italian bro. I have enough room in my heart for you guys."

"And that's why we've been best amigos for five years. Love you loco!"

"Love you more Carlos. See you in a bit!"

An hour later after hopping on the Maine turnpike and then Interstate 95 toward Boston and then Cambridge. I pull up to

Carlos's home on Cedar Street. He has a one-bedroom apartment on the Somerville-Cambridge border not far from the Porter Square T stop. Carlos lives in a three-story cream-colored triple decker on a street lined with elm trees that create shadows in the shape of butterflies on the sidewalks. He has the second floor to himself. I walk up the front stairs and press the buzzer to his unit. He immediately lets me in.

A few seconds later when he opens the door, Carlos greets me with a big warm hug.

"Ladies and gentlemen, he's back from the Arctic Circle! Tommy Perez is back in Boston! Call TMZ!" he declares to an imaginary audience.

"I'm only an hour away, chico. You make it sound like I'm in Alaska or something."

"You might as well be! I think I've seen you more in Miami than I have here since you moved to Greenland, ah, I mean Maine. Same thing, really."

"Well, I'm here now!" I enter his apartment with the ease and familiarity as if it were my own. Over the years, I've crashed on his sofa after one of our late nights at Club Paradise in Kendall Square or House of Blues in Fenway.

I plop myself on his olive-hued sofa and cross my legs on his coffee table where an unopened sweating can of diet soda awaits me. I peel back the tab and listen to the fizz escape before taking a sip. Ahhh!

At the edge of the wooden coffee table is a pile of books, a mix of English literature books that he teaches at Dorchester High as well as some wedding magazines for gays. Carlos and Nick are set to marry in August. That will be necktie #5 for me.

"Wait right there, I want to show you my suit before we head out," Carlos announces before scooting off to his bedroom. Even after all these years, I still think he looks like a younger Josh Grobin but with better styled wavy brown hair. Sometimes, I think Carlos will break out in a thunderous deep baritone voice but the most Carlos can sing is a war-bled tenor in the shower to Lady Gaga. And it's not pretty.

While I wait for Carlos, I leaf through some of the wedding maga-zines. Page and pages of ridiculously good-looking male couples and lipstick lesbians taste-testing cakes or walking hand in hand at one of the resorts that offer special packages.

"*Ta da*, loco!" Carlos breaks my train of thought.

"What do you think?"

I slowly lower the rim of the magazine and appraise Carlos who is sporting a royal blue suit (his favorite color) and pink tie. He twirls around to give me the full effect.

"You look really handsome! Nick is going to love it. That color agrees with you."

"Thanks, loco. We tried different variations, white with red, and black with pink but blue is a great calming color. It reminds me of the ocean and the beaches of Cuba."

Some footnotes on my amigo. Although I was born in Miami, Carlos was born in Cuba and that's something he's extremely proud of. Anyone who visits his apartment walks into a shrine to all things from the island country from vintage tourist posters and a sprawling map to figurines of famous singers such as Celia Cruz. If Carlos could have, he would have been born wrapped in a Cuban flag. He also can't help but end most of his sentences with *Ay Cuba!* Or *Ay this* and *Ay that*! I tease him about that often.

"I think you guys are going to have the perfect wedding in Key West. I can't wait to go. I already have my ticket."

"I've been counting the days. Nick and I thought about doing it up here in Boston but I thought that it would be more meaningful and special to do it in Key West since that's where my family arrived dur-ing the Mariel boatlift. Key West is the closest we can get to Cuba from the US. I want us to be facing south toward my native country. Ay Cuba!" Carlos says his voice rising as his finger stops on Havana on his framed map of the alligator-shaped country.

"Ay Carlos!" I mimic him. "I think that's really sweet. Your ceremony will have a dual meaning."

"What about you, loco? If you could get married anywhere in the world, where would that be?" Carlos says as he returns to his bedroom to change back into his T-shirt and shorts for lunch.

As we talk, I continue leafing through the magazine. Possibilities flash before my eyes. Hawaii.

Provincetown. New York City. Los Angeles. Fort Lauderdale.

"Hmm. I honestly don't know. I think I need a man first!" I shout back to him.

"Ay loco! When you least expect it, it will happen.

But you work so much for the magazine hopping from one story to another that you don't have a lot of time to date. Look at me and Nick. I never saw that coming! Remember, you, me, Nick and Gabriel, Jamaica Plain? We go there now for our anniversary."

Of course I remember the introduction as if it were yesterday. One night, Carlos and I went to another of our culinary hangouts, El Oriental de Cuba Restaurant in Jamaica Plain. We were having our weekly Friday night early dinner of breaded chicken steaks, yucca, rice and black beans (and diet Coke in my case). Just as we were leaving with our bulging stomachs, I bumped into Gabriel Galan, a journalism instructor at Jefferson University in downtown Boston. I was a guest speaker at one of his journalism classes when I was a features reporter at *The Boston Daily.* That night at the restaurant, Gabriel, who always reminded me of an early 40something Latino Roger Federer, happened to be with his best friend Nick, a green-eyed, black-haired Portuguese-Irish middle school teacher, when Gabriel introduced everyone. Immediately, Nick and Carlos connected even though Nick was looking at Carlos like a piece of meat about to be served to a hungry lion. They exchanged phone numbers and began to date. From the start, they realized how much they had in common - school teachers who have a close knit family. They were also the only son in their families. Nick's mom eventually became a second mom for Carlos, whose mother died of colon cancer a year before he moved to Boston.

But it was more than that, Nick's sometimes lack of a filter would make Carlos laugh and Nick seemed to be intrigued by this quiet but sweet handsome lean guy from Miami. I remember Gabriel and I just stood back during the initial introduction as if they were the only ones in the restaurant. Sometimes, you can't explain a connection between two people. It's just there, present and powerful. I'm sure their staring-into-each-other's-eyes contest will repeat itself when they exchange vows at the southern most point of the US. I find it sweet that they remain so entranced with one another. Maybe one day, I will find that again.

Carlos suddenly reappears from his bedroom.

"So my sister and cousins took care of the arrangements and catering. We have our suits. And you should have something written about us. Hint hint! But we've been having trouble finding a photographer. I've been asking around. Do you know of anyone at the magazine or in Miami who could do some freelance work?"

As soon as Carlos said photographer, Danny's handsome face pops into my head.

"Well, funny you should ask. Danny, the photographer at Rico's wedding, did a great job. Check out the photos on my tablet," I say as I whip out my iPad from my messenger bag.

Carlos sits next to me on his sofa and starts to open the photo gallery from Rico's wedding.

I watch Carlos grin as he uses his index finger to swipe through each image.

"I forgot how sexy Rico is but you know what?

These photos show a more vulnerable side. He looks very sweet with Oliver, loco."

"I know, right? Danny saw something that I think most people don't see when they look at the Italian stallion. There's more to him than just his biceps and chest. He has a big heart and Danny homed in on that in the photos."

As Carlos reaches the end of the gallery, he says,

"Well, I'm sold. If this guy can do for Nick and me what he did for Rico and Oliver, then he's our guy. How do I reach him, loco?"

I point to Danny's image and online signature stamp at the end of the gallery.

"He's really handsome. Why didn't you hit that at the wedding?"

"I was the best man, not the best whore. I had duties to fulfill which I took very seriously. Besides, the guy kept barking orders about where to stand and where to look during the photos. That kind of turned me off."

"All that means is that he's a big pussy cat in bed, chico! I say call him up or text him that your other best friend is looking for a photographer. Hey, you may get a date out of it, or some dick! *Ay dick!*" Carlos makes a phallic gesture with his hand and mouth.

I grab one of the wedding magazines and playfully swat Carlos's arm. He breaks out in giggles.

"Or maybe he'll give you a new Facebook profile picture! You could use a new one! Your grays keep coming out! Look in the mirror, old man! " Carlos teases, giggling the whole time as he punches me in the arm.

"Oh yeah! Then maybe I'll have to mention in your wedding poem how much of a POWER BOTTOM you are!" I playfully strike back with one of the sofa pillows.

We go back and forth like this for a few minutes before we head out for lunch like old times.

3

AFTER A HEARTY and carb-filled lunch of tacos and chips at the Border Café with my amigo Mr. Cuban Power Bottom, I steer my VW back to Ogunquit to enjoy the rest of my Saturday. The gleaming mini-forest of Boston skyscrapers recedes from my rear view mirror as I drive over the rickety green and rust-filled Tobin Bridge north toward Interstate 93 and then I-95 toward Maine. As I pass each of the green and white highway signs announcing each town ahead with cars whizzing by with their Massachusetts and New Hampshire plates, I lean my head against my left hand along my Beetle's window. My thoughts return to what Carlos was saying. Where would I want to get married? Who would I want to be there? The latter is easy to answer. I would want to have Rico and Carlos, my dad Pepe and sister Mary and my cousins from Miami. Former co-workers from *The Boston Daily* and my editors and fellow writers from *People*.

The location, well that's another story. All this talk about weddings lately has gotten under my skin but in a good way. It would be nice if I had a necktie for my own wedding instead of the growing collection of ties from everyone else's nuptials. I picture my suit to be a light sky blue hue with a red tie (or pink since that seems to be gay-trendy for weddings.) At the entrance of a reception hall, I picture an HD monitor featuring casual and funny photos of me and my groom. Images of the powdery beaches of Marco Island or Sanibel Island suddenly unfold in my head as I imagine myself standing on a wooden deck facing the aqua green waters of the Gulf of Mexico or the sparkling blue waters off the coast of Maine. I also see myself getting hitched at the top of the Blue Hills just outside Boston as me and my beau look out at the rolling hillside with views of downtown Boston and the harbor in the distance.

My mind continues to drift to the sea, aboard one of those colossal Miami cruise ships where a captain officiates before me and my imaginary groom and our guests as the ship glides into a smear of red and orange during a sunset sail in the Atlantic. But then the cheesy theme song to *The Love Boat* begins to play in my head and the image literally sails away. I smile to myself as I picture the opening credits of the old ABC series with my face in one of the montages: *Special guest star Tommy Perez!* I give into the adventure and sing the song as I continue driving home to The Pine Street State. *The Love Boat...*

As I hum the tune, my smart phone buzzes. It's a text message from Rico in Italy. He should be focusing on his honeymoon, not worrying about me.

With my thumb and index finger (and my eyes on the road), I carefully open the text. There's a picture of a diet Coke can but written in Italian at a bar or a restaurant. The message underneath reads, *I saw this and thought of you, dudette. Having fun on my honeymoon. See you soon in Maine, Boston or somewhere in between. Love, your crazy wingman Rico!"*

I smile as I study the photo and message. Rico took a quick timeout to say Hi. That was so sweet of him. He should be back in a few days and then I can ask him about Danny working as the photographer for Carlos's wedding. I would rather have Rico ask Danny first to see if it would be okay to connect him with Carlos for his wedding rather than me awkwardly emailing him out of the blue. I wouldn't want the guy to think I was hitting on him or anything. As I approach the Massachusetts New Hampshire border by Portsmouth, I quickly text Rico back, *Eat a lot of pasta for me in Italy. Miss you amigo!*

A few hours later, I decide to shake off all the wedding stuff. I'm going out tonight in Ogunquit even though options are limited. The town is about four miles long after all. I was thinking of stopping by the Front Porch which has an outdoor bar and a piano bar but I rather go where they might be younger guys and more current music. So my first stop or everyone's first or last stop is MaineStreet, a bar and club with a second-floor roof deck with views of city streets. Unlike Boston where snobby attitudes can rule the club scene at times, the bars in Maine are open and friendly where everyone is welcomed. People casually strike up a conversation as easily as they light up a match for you.

That's one of the things that I appreciate about my adopted home – the ease and friendliness people say Hi and engage with you as if you're old friends. You could be in the lobby of the historical Ogunquit Playhouse, our main cultural institution, or at one of the charming Victorian-themed inns or sitting on a bench along Marginal Way and Mainers genuinely seem to want to chat with you and get to know you. I quite haven't figured out why. Maybe because life hums to a different rhythm here. The hustle and bustle of the nearest downtown, which is Portland, is an hour away and even that metropolis is tiny compared to Boston or New York City. There's something about the salt-laced air, the fragrance of tall pines and the cool breezes that seems to sedate tensions in Maine which makes this artist colony and village a beautiful respite for families and creative types particularly during the summer. When I stroll down Beach Street and pass a set of weathered brown clapboard apartments, I enjoy standing at the edge of the small bridge where I marvel at the crystal clear blue water that flows beyond the bridge. When I walk some more toward the beach after the wind-swept restaurants and old-school inns, I stand at the beach's edge and I gaze out at the ocean and I see infinity, an ever-expanding sense of possibility. I breathe in the ocean air and my deadline pressures from the magazine wash away with the waves into the northern Atlantic.

A few hours later, it's just past 9 p.m. and I catch my reflection on the glass front window of a bakery as I stride toward MaineStreet in the center of town off Route 1. The latest pop music floats from the bar and out into the street as I climb a few steps inside where a crowd of mostly men in shorts and Polos and loose fitting T-shirts dances in place and mingles with their drinks. The chatter mixes with the pop music and the laughter from the dance floor as the guys pump their fists in the air and groove to the music.

As I approach the counter to order a vodka with Diet Coke from the bartender, I hear a familiar voice coming from a small stage near the dance floor. Oh no! It's the one and only...

"*Yoo hoo!* Hello everybody! My name is Kyle but you probably already knew that from my MTV days. I'm your special guest host here tonight, the main attraction at MaineStreet and I want to welcome everyone on this fabulous Saturday night," he says with a feminine lisp while laughing at his own joke.

He continues to introduce the hunky bartenders who nod or wave back from their stations.

For non-MTV viewers, Kyle is a tall, lean and preening former reality TV model who has managed to extend his 15 minutes of fame into a few years thanks to guest spots on MTV challenges and providing delicious sound bites on VH1 during their weekend pop culture round ups.

When he's not on TV, this statuesque dirty-blonde haired and blue-eyed guy, who looks like the male version of actress Jennifer Lawrence, tours bars in New England and South Florida to host special themed nights and events. I actually know the dude.

I met him a few years ago in Boston just after his first season on *The Real World*. I wrote a profile on him for the newspaper and our website and that seemed to unfortunately endear him to me ... for life! He hasn't spotted me - yet. But he will. It's hard to miss Mr. KY (his nickname on the reality show after a sloppy threesome episode that involved a lot of lubricant. If you need to know more about that, read my profile online or go to Kyle's Wikipedia page.

"MaineStreet is an Ogunquit tradition. No, scratch that. A Maine summer institution and I feel so honored to be here with you all. As you mingle and cruise and you know you will and your welcomed to mingle and cruise with yours truly by the way, I will be occasionally coming up to the stage to introduce a local musician who will play a set. So without further adieu, let me introduce fellow Maine reality star Joe Adams who appeared as a finalist on last year's *The Voice* on NBC. Let's give Joe a big warm Maine welcome. Bravo! Bravo! Bravo!" Kyle announces. He places the microphone back on its stand and makes room for the reality TV singer, an Adam Levine wanna-be.

As Kyle steps down, a handsome gentleman to my right smiles and holds up his drink.

"To Maine!" he says, his olive-colored eyes twinkling from his tanned face. Mystery man has short, groomed salt and pepper hair cut into a tight-fade on the sides almost like a military buzz cut.

I look down at my drink, smile and take a sip.

"Ditto!" I say sheepishly.

"Hey, are you from here? I'm new in town. By the way, my name is Ignacio," he says, with a slight Spanish-accent as he takes a swig of his beer. His eyes intensely bore into mine.

"Nice to meet you. I'm Tommy Perez! I live here but I'm actually from Boston, well Miami to be exact. Long story. I've moved around but this is my home. Nice to meet you."

I smile as he firmly shakes my hand.

"What about you?"

"I moved here after Memorial Day. I'm helping a friend run his inn. I guess you can say I'm the assistant manager. You may know the place. OH."

"Oh?" I say, somewhat confused.

"OH!" Ignacio repeats.

"Huh?"

"Sorry, Tommy. I thought you knew. It's Ogunquit House. We call it OH."

"Ah...okay," I say, playfully hitting my hand on my forehead.

"We take pets, too!"

"That's good to know, if I ever get a pet," I joke. "Welcome to Maine, Ignacio."

We're standing along the bar when the bartender returns with my drink. I nod and pay him the $6. (That's another thing I like Maine. Drinks are cheaper than in Boston.)

"A handsome young man like you shouldn't be left alone. What are you doing so far away from Miami?" Ignacio takes another swig of his drink. I notice a colorful sun tattoo on his left wrist.

I like that he called me handsome. My cheeks instantly flush at the word young. I just turned 40 but people have told me that I can pass for early 30s because of my slight build and dark brown curly hair (which I sometimes dye to hide the gray invasion. Don't tell!)

I go on and quickly tell Ignacio my back story, that I was a reporter in Miami who relocated to Boston a few years ago to write for *The Boston Daily* and now I cover everyday people doing interesting things or celebrities doing pretty much anything for *People* mag.

"That's great, Tommy. I read the magazine. We have a subscription at the inn. I'll have to look for your name now," he says, again smiling which makes his eyes crinkle. Because of the lines and salt and peppered hair, I suspect he's about mid to late 40s. Ignacio has that Scott Bakula look, sun-tanned, sinewy but masculine. Some black hairs poke out from the top of his short-sleeved green shirt which compliments his eyes. As I visually appraise him, I'm suddenly aroused, a tingly thrilly rush stirs within me. Maybe pheromones? Or maybe it's the alcohol beginning to course through my system? I don't know but his Spanish Antonio-Banderas accent makes me curious. Where is he from? Does it really matter? *Me gusta!*

"Um, I notice you have an accent. I'm sorry for pointing that out but I grew up with accents so I'm curious, where are you from, Ignacio? I can't seem to place it." I take a slurp of my drink and continue looking at him.

"Ahhh, my accent. It's a conversation starter in this town. Everyone else here has the Boston or New Hampshire accent. I'm from Costa Rica originally. I went to college in Oklahoma and studied business and then worked at a hotel as an accountant in Orlando. I've moved around a bit too and my accent seems to follow me wherever I go," he says with a half smile. I smile back at the joke.

"I think accents are beautiful. They tell the world where we're from," I say, realizing how cheesy that must have sounded.

Ignacio lets out a small laugh.

"You're really cute Mr. Tommy Perez," he says, clinking his beer bottle to my glass. I smile and look down and then up at his dark greenish eyes.

We stand along our little section of the bar staring and smiling at one another when Kyle returns to the stage and thanks the reality TV singer for his cover song of Maroon Five's *This Love* which nobody seemed to listen to including Ignacio and me. The guys were too busy checking each other out on the dance floor, at the bar counters or in the bathroom.

"Joe is going to take a little break at the bar right over there," Kyle says, pointing my way.

His eyes light up when he spots me. "Feel free to stop and say Hi to him or to moi. I'll be back shortly. In the meantime, enjoy the music of our house deejay, people!" Kyle says, stepping down from the stage.

And like a shark fin locking onto some gay prey ahead, Kyle makes a bee-line toward me. As Carlos would say, *Ay no!* It's too late to make a run for the front door. I'm stuck here and I can't escape. Ignacio turns to me.

"Do you know that guy, Tommy? He's coming straight toward you like he's a man on a mission," Ignacio says, his eyes wide and full of concerned. A little smirk curls up from his lips.

"Um yeah, that's Kyle. He's hard to miss, like right now."

And before I could say another word...

"TOMMY PEREZ! OH...MY...GOD! How are you?" he says, leaning down to give me a big hug which lifts me off my feet. He then greets me with a flurry of insincere lip brushes on both sides of my face.

"Good, Mr. KY, I mean Kyle," I squeak out from the octopus-like embrace.

"I haven't seen you in ages since you, wait, you're not in Boston anymore because I haven't seen you out in FOR-E-V-E-R!" he says, inviting himself to take a sip of my drink.

Ignacio watches the spectacle with a bigger smirk on his chiseled face.

"Well, I live here now, Kyle. Maine is my home." Kyle's blue eyes bug out from my news.

"In Maine? But por que? You were like Boston's favorite Cuban son! No, you were the Bay State's prodigal Cuban son! You were my favorite Latino in Boston and maybe the only one for that matter."

"Thanks Kyle. I think. I wanted to get away from the Hub. I wanted a slower pace of living and my job allows me to work from home," I say, taking control of my drink again which Kyle mostly slurped.

"Who are you writing for these days, the Portland paper?"

"Nope. People."

"What people are you talking about?" Kyle says, turning his head, looking around the bar to see if anyone is checking him out.

"I mean, People magazine. I'm a New England-based correspondent," I declare proudly. I hand him one of my business cards.

At the mention of the word People, Kyle's eyes light up like the bright beam of a New England lighthouse.

"Oh wow! That's PER-fect! Now you can write about me... AGAIN! Maybe a celebrity-sighting feature. Kyle was seen frolicking on the beaches of Ogunquit with a handsome mystery man," he says, in third person, tapping Ignacio's lean chest with his index finger which surprises Ignacio. My eyebrows furrow and I narrow my eyes at Kyle as if to telegraph for him to back off. I saw him first. Kyle picks up on my cue and continues gabbing.

"Or you can do a follow up on ME now that I'm a pop culture diva on TV."

"Well...." I say, trying to think of a way out of this. "We'll see. If you marry a famous celebrity up here, I'd probably cover the nuptials for the magazine or at least online. Weddings are like my sub-beat so get to work on finding a groom!" I snap my fingers playfully.

"I'll work overtime on that, Tommy. Now if you and your amigo will please excuse me, I have to get back on stage and back to work. See you around!" Kyle announces, throwing a few perfunctory air kisses in my general direction.

He then flicks his index finger on Ignacio's green T-shirt. Before Kyle leaves, he turns my way and silently mouths, "He's hot. Go for it Tommy! Sorry for interrupting!"

I grin at Kyle whose attention is already diverted by another club goer who is eyeing him. I bid adieu to Kyle, for now. My eyes roll back and I exhale loudly which makes Ignacio laugh.

As the crowds flow in out and out of the bar like the waves from Ogunquit Beach, I remain here chatting with his handsome stranger.

"Tommy, do you want to go upstairs to the deck? You can see the inn from up there," Ignacio says.

"Sure!" I say, as he begins to escort me upstairs. As we climb the wooden stairs, he gently places his left hand on my upper back.

"As long as we don't see Kyle,' I joke on the way. Once we arrive, we take our perch along the wooden railing and gaze up at the starry black Maine sky which is lighted by the dim glow of a sliver moon. The lights of the town wink back at us as if they approve of this sweet scene. As we talk about his work from dealing with customer complaints to scheduling the house keepers and how much he loves to read historical fiction, I occasionally glance at Ignacio's sun tattoo. I want to reach out and touch it because I imagine that it would feel nice and warm. The ocean breeze makes a rainbow flag sail enthusiastically in front of the bar. I know the feeling.

4

THE SUN IS high in the sky as I pull up to the majestic idyllic grounds of the Kripalu Center for Yoga and Health in Stockbridge in western Massachusetts. It's Monday morning and I've been driving for more than two hours to get here from Maine.

Such is the life of a roving reporter with such a big coverage area. My assignment for today – a feature on the growing popularity of Broga. Haven't heard of it? Neither did I before the assignment landed in my lap. It's yoga for bros. Really. That's why I'm writing about it for the magazine. The class touts itself as "You don't even have to touch your toes!" We'll see about that.

It's a retreat for guys looking to stretch themselves so to speak but some women also partake in the classes which have spectacular views of Lake Mahkeenac across the rolling hilly woodlands. Picture pony-tail wearing lean guys and women in yoga pants or jump suits and you have the majority of the participants at Kripalu, at least that's what I gathered from the website.

The center offers various yoga classes as well as kayaking, hiking excursions (which I would like to do sometime when I'm not working) and spa amenities such as massages and facials. But for the magazine, I need to write a punchy 600 word feature on Broga. It would appeal to our core readers, mostly women who may be interested in hearing about the trend to get their husbands or boyfriends off the couch. The idea is to practice traditional yoga movements with familiar exercises to get into shape.

The focus is on the back, shoulders, arms and chest. The class is basically a gentler boot camp. Out-of-shape dudes and the flexibility-challenged learn the basics of yoga. Broga, here I come!

It's just past 10 a.m. and one of the classes is about to begin when I walk inside a grand open room filled with streaming sunlight, bathing the room in a golden hue. The back wall of windows provides views of the rolling hills pocked with fir and spruce trees. About 10 guys who range in age from mid-20s to 50s, stand before Chris, the instructor with a collection of flowing dreadlocks that highlight his olive skin. The center manager had given the staff the heads up that I and a photographer would be hanging around and taking notes. As I look around the room, I smile and wave to the instructor and the guys who are lined up in rows before me.

"Welcome to broga, brogis! We have a special visitor with us today. Tommy Perez is a writer for *People* magazine and he'll be observing us today. Let's welcome him everyone!"

The guys say Hi, nod or wave my way.

"He may want to interview some of you after the class so if you can stick around for a few minutes, that would be great. It's great PR for the center."

"Just forget that I'm here. I'm a fly on the wall. I swear!" I say as I squat in the corner and make myself comfortable.

Chris opens the class by reading some inspirational quotes followed by Namaste. He then gently guides the guy to pose like animals and warriors. All I see are rows of hairy arms and legs. Immediately, a chorus of groans erupts.

I hear some bones crack. Faces turn crimson. Heavy breathing ensues but everyone soldiers on. I grin as I scribble everything down. As Chris continues with more stretching exercises, I wonder, where is the photographer?

Patty, my assignment editor, told me yesterday that the magazine had hired a local freelance photographer. Someone named Donny or something.

"You don't have to touch your toes. Just do your best. *Feel* the burn. Go with the flow. *Yesss*," Chris encourages everyone with his soothing surfer-like voice as some guys look up with furrowed eyebrows. Sweat drips from their noses onto their colorful yoga mats. I don't know if it's the sunlight or the body heat but it's beginning to feel stuffy in here like a high school gym.

"Maybe we can get Tommy Perez to do some poses!" Chris suddenly announces as he looks up from his dog pose.

"Um, that's okay. I don't think I'm all that, um, brotastic. I rather watch and take notes."

The other guys egg me on.

"Come on, Tommy! If you're going to write about us, you might as well try it," says one 30something year-old guy with a fuzzy crew cut, green eyes and beer belly. He sports a Red Sox blue headband.

"Yeah, man!" another guy chimes in.

"Get him on the mat, Chris!" another dude in his 50s with a receding hairline shouts. I wish he and the others would shut up and focus on their poses.

"Tommy, I think the class has spoken. Will you join us, please?" Chris says, pulling out a mat for me and a pair of green shorts with the center's logo.

Oh no! My eyes widen and my mouth turns into a big black hole. The class has put me on the spot. If I don't join in, they may not chat with me afterward. I'll look like a bad sport and make the magazine look bad. Naturally, I cave in, mentally throwing my hands up in the air. I'll be a brogi for the morning, just this once.

"Okay, okay. I'm in. I'll participate. But can I get an Ommm?" I joke, as I grab the shorts from Chris. Luckily, I happen to be wearing a loose fitting blue cotton T-shirt so I'll blend with the guys and scenery.

I step into a nearby bathroom, quickly change and return to the class and remove my sneakers.

I don't want to make an ass out of myself so I plop myself in the rear of the room where everyone's rear stares back at me seemingly taunting me. Chris continues leading the class. Although I hike and run, I rarely stretch so there's a sudden burning pain in my hips and calves as I position myself into a warrior pose.

This...is...not...welcomed. Argh. This is what an arthritic rhino must feel like.

As we shift into another position which resembles a human table, I glance up at Chris and the sea of butts when someone walks into class. I squint to make sure I am seeing who I am seeing. I recognize the black wavy hair, the blue eyes, the square jaw, the cocky swagger. It's Danny, Rico's wedding photographer. He spots me, wiggles his eyebrows and starts aiming his camera my way while I look like I'm about to break in half from all the bending and stretching.

"Hey everyone, this must be the photographer!" Chris announces.

"Just call me Danny. I promise to make everyone look good. Promise!" he says in a charming tone while looking at me with a steely stare. I think his lip just curled up a bit. He's enjoying this. I know that Carlos and Rico would get a kick of me seeing me in this position, propped up on all fours.

Danny's camera clicks as he walks around the class while we move into a cow pose, which involves us looking up as we're propped up on arms and legs.

As he approaches me, he quickly stops and points the camera in my face.

"SMILE TOMMY!" he shouts and then laughs as I look up into the lens. My face cringes at the thought that Danny has captured me as I angle down while my butt is high up in the air, ready for...well let's not go there. This is called the downward dog but I feel like I'm in a yoga porno as I bend into these all these exhausting and sexually suggestive poses.

I level a straight-face expression at him but a slight smirk betrays me.

"Um, thanks Danny. You know I can't be in the photos. The story is about the class. Not me. It's called PEOPLE. Not Tommy!"

"Yeah, I know. Just having some fun with you. You're an easy target. It looks like you like that position. You're pretty good at it." He takes more photos of me. I squint and return my focus to the Broga.

During the rest of the class, my body cracks and makes noises I've never heard before except for a fart (it slipped out, sorry) during the cobra pose. Luckily, no one heard my rear from the rear of the class. Like a human drone, Danny hovers around the room with his camera capturing every angle and pretzel-like pose that we attempt. I don't think writers are intended for all this body-bending and holding positions in ways our bodies aren't naturally inclined to doing. Why would I ever be in a downward dog pose? Never mind. The only things that should bend from my body are my fingers – over a keyboard.

At the end of the class, Chris guides us to close our eyes and to deeply i-n-h-a-l-e and e-x-h-a-l-e as we sit in an easy pose. That's yoga speak for legs crossed over one another. We hold our hands up in prayer and connect with a higher being. Besides the collective heavy breathing, the only other sound I hear is Danny's camera firing away. I open my right eye and catch Danny staring back at me and smiling. He silently mouths, "Close your eyes!" and I shut my eye and grin.

And then Chris declares, "Namaste."

I rise and stretch, shake my head side to side to make sure it's still attached. Chris thanks me and shakes my hand. I grab my notepad and interview some of the guys about the experience. Like me, their shirts are drenched and their faces are flushed. Most of the guys said they would do this again. They feel relaxed and reinvigorated. I scribble everything down as my sweat dampens my notepad.

Within half an hour, I'm done. I gather my shoes and messenger bag which has my pair of jeans when Danny slowly approaches me with a victorious grin.

"I think I'm all set. I got a group shot as well as individual shots of the guys with the hills in the background. Oh, and I have some of you too. Should I post those on People.com or send to Grindr or Scruff? I'm sure the guys there would appreciate your ability to get down on all fours."

"Ha ha! Not funny but if there is a good photo of me not looking like a sweaty pig or barn animal, please email it to me. I can always post it on my Facebook or Instagram and share it with my friends," I say, looking into the small black pupils of Danny's aquatic-blue eyes. My, he's so handsome and yet kind of jerk at the same time or maybe that's how he is with people – he makes fun of them to the point of annoying them.

"Tommy, hey it was good seeing you. I'll send you a photo this afternoon. I'd stick around and hang out but I am off to another assignment. Life of a freelancer!" he says, patting me on my upper shoulder. "See ya around."

Then, I suddenly, I remember that I need to ask him about Carlos's wedding later this summer.

"Danny, wait. Before you go, I want to ask you something. My other best friend in Boston, Carlos, is getting married in Key West in August and he's looking for a good photographer. He liked the photos you took at Rico and Oliver's wedding and well, he wanted me to reach out to you on his behalf. Can I forward him your information, in case you're looking for extra summer work?" Danny's face softens. A genuine smile plays at the corners of his mouth.

"Sure! I love shooting weddings, something I enjoy doing on the side when I'm not working on news stories or family portraits. It's the most important day in a couple's life so yeah, feel free to forward my info to your friend. I'd love to help out if the scheduling works." He hands me one of his cards.

"Thanks Danny. I really appreciate it and I know Carlos will too."
I study the card which has Danny's handsome face behind a camera
lens.

"Hey, anything for a friend of Rico. See you around," he says, with
a wink before leaving the classroom.

"Yeah, see you soon, maybe."

About half an hour later after changing back into my jeans, splash-
ing my face with water from the bathroom and drinking lime-flavored
water in the lobby, I'm still feeling all Zenned out. I'm walking out
of the center toward my Volkswagen when my smart phone pings.
There's a new email.

When I open the attachment, it's a photo of me laughing and
looking to the side. I'm standing with my hands pressed together in
prayer in front of the giant glass windows with views of the green
hills in the background. I stare at the photo and smile. Danny really
captured me in a fun moment during the class. I actually look good,
really good. This is definitely going on Facebook and Instagram. The
email is signed, "Here you go, Brogi Tommy!"

I save the photo and respond, "Thanks Danny!" and I immediately
post it on my accounts with the tag line, *Another fun day at work.*

Carlos instantly comments on Facebook: *Oye loco, great photo. I
can't even see your grays! LOL*

And then Rico follows up and writes, *Hey buddy, since when do
you take Yoga? Good photo though.. Who took the photo? Call me later
with the details!*

I smile at their comments and at the sudden number of likes that
the photo attracts. I also immediately respond to Rico that Danny
was the photographer.

As I drive back to Ogunquit to write my story, I also decide to
quickly text the image to Ignacio, the handsome guy I met the other
night.

I text him, *In case you're wondering what I'm writing about for the next issue of the magazine, here's a preview. Here's to a happy Monday, Ignacio!*

He instantly texts me back, *So handsome! It was great chatting with you Saturday. I was just thinking about you. Drinks soon?*

I type back, *Sure. I can show you my new Broga moves!*

Broga? Is that a new dance? he writes back.

Nah, it's a long story. I'll explain when we meet up. ☺

5

"LOCO, SO HE said yes. Danny is going to shoot my wedding. And he's not as expensive as I thought which is even better. Thank you so much!" Carlos greets me over the phone.

"Well, I'm glad it worked out. Are you meeting him beforehand to discuss what you want from the photos? What angles, group photos, etc?" I ask, spritzing some cologne in my bathroom. I'm almost done getting ready to meet up with Ignacio on this Friday night.

"Yeah, we're meeting next week so I'll keep you posted. What are you doing tonight? I hear some water running in the background, loco."

I tell him about having a drink and some dinner with Ignacio at The Front Porch.

"Finally, a date! Whoo hoo! I was worried about you there for a little while. You haven't dated...IN MONTHS! Even the nuns in Boston get more action than you, loco."

"You may be right about that. The priests too! But this guy was so nice the other night we met and he can hold a conversation. He's a great listener too. It doesn't hurt that he looks like a younger Scott Bakula."

"Who's that, loco?"

"You know, the actor who was on that old show *Quantum Leap* where he traveled in different points of time. Okay, maybe you're too young for that show.

He had a small role in the gay HBO series *Looking*. He's also on *NCIS New Orleans* on CBS. He leads the team."

I hear Carlos typing in the background on his laptop.

"Okay Mr. TV Guide. I just found him. Oh wow, super guapo. Remember, take it slow. It's just one date. Have fun and don't drink too many vodkas with diet Cokes. You can get a little flirty-sloppy after a few drinks and you know what I'm talking about. *Hmmm-mmm*."

I feign offense.

"Um excuse you, loca! I get giddy and I never have more than two drinks because I'm always the one who has to drive. In fact, I'm walking to the bar. This is Ogunquit. You can get everywhere by foot or bike."

"And don't talk too much about your OCD and Mikey. Your OCD will be obvious once he sits down with you and you start twirling your straw paper or napkin or your curly hair. No guy wants to hear about another guy's ex on the first date. He's your past, not your present and definitely not your future. Focus on this guy. What was his name again, loco?"

"Ignacio!" I blurt out, while plucking my eyebrows.

"Does he speak Spanish?"

"Si! He's from Costa Rica originally."

"Well, I like him already. Maybe we can all have a double date if tonight goes well or you can bring him to the wedding this summer. Remember, don't – "

"I know," I interrupt Carlos. "I'll watch what I drink and say and I won't mention the M-word. I love you!"

"Love you too, loco! And I want to hear everything tomorrow!"

"Of course! I'll call you first thing in the morning."

After I place my smartphone down on top of my beige bathroom sink, I quickly give myself a once over in the mirror. My dark brown curly hair looks groomed for once. My black thick eyebrows appear symmetrical thanks to the tweezing. One time, I over plucked one side and I looked as if I was suspicious of everything because the right brow arched higher than the other. I remember Rico telling me once, "Will you stop looking at me like that? It's like your questioning everything I am telling you."

It's a good thing that eyebrow hairs grows back fast, hence my twice-a-week plucking sessions in my bathroom. We Latinos, we hairy!

I button up my short-sleeved, baby-blue shirt which matches my brown shorts and I flash a big smile and a two thumbs up in the mirror. I spritz some more cologne and create a haze. *Cough cough!* I grab my olive wind breaker just in case of a sudden Maine rain and I stride out the door.

As soon as I walk under the yellow awnings of the Front Porch about ten minutes later, I spot Ignacio. He's sitting at a corner bar table in the lounge area by the piano bar. He grins when he spots me. I smile back as I take in the lusty-dreamy sight – olive-green eyes, short salt-and-pepper hair, Polo shirt with some chest hairs poking out from the collar. Strong veins run down his muscular tanned and freckled arms. He holds up a glass as he walks toward me and hugs me.

"Hola señor Tommy Perez!" he says in his Spanish accent. "So good to see you. You look so handsome. Here, I ordered you a drink. A vodka with Diet Coke, right?"

I nod and smile as I hug him back. He remembered my drink. I'm tickled by the gesture.

"Thank you, Ignacio. You have a good memory," I say taking a seat at the bar table and offering to buy him a drink but then I notice that he already has a fruity cocktail.

"To People magazine and all your wonderful stories. I just read Broga online. Good job. Your writing is very descriptive and I could hear your voice when I read the article," he says, taking a sip of his drink.

My cheeks suddenly warm. I'm flattered that he took the time to find the article online before this weekend's print publication.

"Thanks Ignacio. I try to make my stories as chatty as I can. They should read like you're sitting with me having a conversation or eavesdropping on one."

"I definitely could see that," he says opening the menu. "It was a fun read. Maybe, I should try Broga some time! Would you want to do it with me, Tommy?"

"Thanks but I think that was my first and last time at attempting Broga. I'm done with animal poses and turning myself into a human pretzel. I'll stick to hiking. You're welcome to come with me the next time I go. You can see another side of Maine or New Hampshire or Boston. One of my favorite places there is called the Blue Hills."

"Are the Blue Hills sad?" Ignacio says with a playful frown which makes me smile. I like that he has a sense of humor or at least he tries. He gets an A for effort. There's a certain sexy cadence in his voice, almost lyrical. He speaks English with a Spanish intonation like so many guys in Miami. It reminds me of the hot guys at home.

"Um, no, they're not sad but they're really cool. Actually they're called the Blue Hills because once upon a time, many moons ago, the early explorers thought they looked blue from their ships. From certain angles and the way the sun hits the hills, they look, well blue from a distance. That's how the name came about. But once you're there, it's all green and granite rocks."

"Well, you have to show me sometime, Tommy," he says hopefully. He smiles, which radiates a certain sunniness and warmth.

I smile and look down at one of the red rectangular menus on my table and open it.

A few moments later, a tanned, buffed and bald waiter appears and takes our orders. I ask for a turkey club sandwich with chips. Ignacio asks for the grilled chicken sandwich and another drink.

"Thank you, gentlemen. Your order will be right up," the waiter says before disappearing into the swirl of activity in the kitchen.

I twirl my straw into a mini tornado. I smile as Ignacio leans in closer over the table and I do the same.

"So... tell me about Costa Rica. To be honest, I don't know much about the place except that I think that's where one of the Jurassic Parks was filmed or where the first book was based."

Ignacio tilts his head back and laughs.

"You're right, Tommy. But there is much more to my country than a being back drop to Steven Spielberg's dinosaurs."

Ignacio's eyes then carry a faraway look as he begins to talk about his home country.

"Costa Rica is beautiful. We have lush mountains, beautiful beaches where I used to surf as a teenager. You walk along the roads and you hear a chorus of wild birds and monkeys. Sometimes, the monkeys steal your food from your plate if you eat outside. That used to happen to me a lot," he laughs quietly. As he talks, my eyes glance down at the sun tattoo on his wrist. Again, I want to touch it and know more about it and what it means.

"We like to say that being there is *pura vida* because life there is as pure as you can get or there is plenty of life. There is much wildlife there and because of the universal health care system and low-cost of living, you can have a nice good life there. I would love to go back and retire there some day."

"If it's so great, why did you leave? I think I would have stayed there even if the monkeys stole my plates of turkey sandwiches," I say, taking a sip of my drink picturing everything that Ignacio described.

"My job moved me to Miami and then Orlando. I was moving up the corporate ladder at the hotel chain. All I did was work, work and work. With every new management position, I had less time at home. I was practically living at the hotels. In Orlando last year, I was burning out fast. I had to go work on the weekends whenever the hotel's owner and associates visited. The executives also had to participate in boot camp after work. And there were morning work breakfasts and weekend community events that we were required to attend several times a month. And the last week of the month is always the worst because of the financials. I prepared the budgets and it was a never-ending process. Long story short, I left Costa Rica because of my job and I left Orlando because I needed a break. When a friend of mine asked me to help manage his inn here in Ogunquit, I instantly felt relaxed. Less stress, easier job, and a new environment. Besides, I hear they do Broga here," Ignacio says with a wink.

"Yeah, I hear it's catching on," I say, widening my eyes.

"And as beautiful as Costa Rica is, it's still a third world country. The infrastructure needs updating. Many of the roads are paved but they are in bad shape or too narrow and many of the streets don't have signs. We know how to get from one to place to another by landmarks, like a big fig tree or the building next to the building down from the post office. But at least we have Starbucks!"

"Yeah, they're everywhere, kind of like Dunkin' Donuts in Boston. One on every corner! When lost, look for the orange and pink sign and you'll be on your way."

The waiter suddenly returns with our plates of food and sets them before us. We begin to chow down. In between bites, we continue talking. The conversation flows easily and naturally like a waterfall. I wonder if they have those too in Costa Rica? I wonder how Ignacio looks shirtless under a waterfall. I imagine water cascading all over his lean hairy chest as he leans back against a rock while running his hands through his hair.

"Tommy, Tommy, are you still with me? Hello! " Ignacio says which draws me out of my gay daydream. He looks at me with a penetrating gaze.

"Yes, sorry. I was just picturing…Costa Rica! So, what do you do for fun, Ignacio besides read fabulously-written articles by Cuban-American journalists in Maine?" I say, dabbing the corners of my mouth with a napkin.

"I'm with Amiga!"

"Who's Amiga? Does she also live in Ogunquit?"

"Yes, she does. She lives with me at the inn. She can be a little too affectionate sometimes, always trying to kiss me everywhere we go."

"Um, okay," I say, imagining an overly-affectionate fag hag, girlfriend.

"I think it's great that you have a friend in town. You have some-one to come home to and hang out and talk about your day with."

"Well, she doesn't talk but I can read her well. I know what's she thinking with just one look."

"Oh my God, is she mute?" My eyes bug out and Ignacio starts laughing in an Anderson Cooper-kind of way.

"My apologies. I should have been clearer. Amiga is like my family. I take care of her."

"I kinda figured that. You two sound very close."

Ignacio keeps laughing.

"Tommy, you don't understand. Amiga is my –"

"Girlfriend? That explains it. You're involved with a woman and you date men on the side. I get it. There are a lot of you in Maine, Boston and Miami to be exact. It's pretty common."

I click my tongue and shake my head disapprovingly.

"Nooo, Tommy. Let me explain. Amiga is my –"

"Beard! You don't need to explain. And then people wonder why I'm single because gay men have fake girlfriends or wives and they're unavailable and I rather have a guy to myself and not share so go figure!"

Ignacio can't stop from laughing. He slaps his knee with his right hand. He then grabs my right hand and squeezes.

A sudden rush of tingles runs up my spine.

"Do you ever stop talking, Mr. Perez? Amiga is my little dog, my little perrita," he blurts out before I interrupt him again.

I sit there with my straw dangling from the side of my mouth. Oh my Gosh!

I don't know what to say. Carlos was right. I'm saying stupid things and I've barely had one drink. In my defense, the drink is strong and I'm feeling giddy-buzzy. I suck at dates. I'm also pretty sure that I've sucked some dates. Besides Mikey, my longest relationship has been with my body pillow and at least that doesn't let me down.

"Oh, that's cute! You have a dog! Do you have a picture?"

He grins which makes his eyes crinkle in a sexy way. He pulls out his smartphone. The screen saver is a picture of a snow-white Fox terrier with big black and brown ears that stand up. She is actually staring at the camera as if posing. Wicked cute.

Ignacio hands me his phone and he quickly thumbs through a slide show of her photos. Amiga is adorable. With my index finger and thumb, I expand some of the photos which show her running on the beach, holding a tennis ball in her mouth and sitting on his lap and looking up at the camera. Another photo has her sporting big pink sunglasses. Amiga could easily be a cute cartoon character. Amiga the explorer!

I tilt my head to the side and smile at Ignacio who beams with pride as she shows off Amiga as if she were his fur daughter. It's endearing. I'm definitely liking this guy. I wonder if he shows the same kind of pride with boyfriends.

"Amiga is very needy because she used to stay home alone most of the day when I worked those long hours at the hotels. It wasn't fair to her or to me. At least here in this new job, I live at the inn and I check up on her throughout the day and take her for walks. She is much happier. So am I," he says, his voice carrying a certain calmness which is infectious. Maine has that effect on people except during the arctic winter. For some reason, I feel so relaxed around Ignacio, at ease.

There's no pressure. Just good conversation. It doesn't hurt that I can't keep my eyes off Mr. Sweet and Sexy. Those hairs poking out from his collar are giving me unpure *pura vida* thoughts.

"I always wanted a dog but all the places that I've lived in didn't allow them. So I like to think of my friends' dogs as my own. I'm like their godfather. I'd love to meet Amiga some time!"

"Of course, how about after our dinner and drinks? We can take her for a walk along Marginal Way and look at the ocean. There's a specific bench where she likes to sniff a lot. I'm sure she'll like you, Tommy Perez. You can be her Amigo," he says with a wink. My heart melts at the thought of meeting this ham of a dog. I want to be Ignacio's amigo too. Actually, I want to be more than just a friend.

"On that note, let's make a toast, Ignacio!" I say, holding up my dwindling supply of vodka and Diet Coke. He holds up his fruity cocktail.

"To new amigos in Maine!" I say.

"To pura vida!" he says, clinking his glass back to mine. Our eyes lock and I grin. Where is this going? I don't know but I'm enjoying going with the pura vida flow.

6

AFTER OUR DINNER and drinks, Ignacio and I stroll along Route 1. The air is cool and breezy as we pass fellow residents and tourists milling about and walking to and from the cafes, galleries and shops that line the main artery.

We take a short side street to Marginal Way where the moonlight shimmers against the Atlantic Ocean making it look like a blanket of crystals. Small sail boats, lighted by their lamps, gently bob in the distance. The wind blows through my hair and I can feel it standing up or tilting lopsided. I smush it down with my right hand repeatedly, one of my habits in this windy town.

"Don't worry about your hair, handsome," Ignacio says as we stride side to side along the paved cliff walk. Other couples do the same and stroll with their arms linked.

"That's easy for you to say. Your hair doesn't move at all in this weather. You're being too sweet. My hair mushrooms into a giant Chia Pet with any little gust of wind," I say with a laugh. I don't want to look like a cheap decorative plant in front of Ignacio. I want to look good for him.

We arrive at the rear of his workplace, a stately three-story Victorian inn surrounded by manicured bright green lawns like so many other businesses, homes and residence buildings nearby.

"Want to come inside for a little bit? I'm going to get Amiga," he says with a warm inviting grin.

"Sure! Lead the way!"

He places his right hand on my upper back as we walk up the brick steps of the inn which is flanked with mini wooden barrels filled with yellow, white and purple impatiens and bright red and pink pansies.

Once inside, a front clerk in her mid-20s greets Ignacio with a big smile.

"Hola Ignacio! Como estas?" she says in her Americanized Spanish as if she were a first-year student.

"Muy bien, Michelle. Estas hablando español muy bien! Te presento a mi amigo Tommy Perez."

"Hi Michelle! Nice to meet you!" I wave to the friendly brunette with hazel eyes in the lobby which has shiny wooden floors and a spewing small fountain.

"Nice to meet you too. Welcome to our little inn!" she says with a quick wave, returning her focus back to her computer monitor.

We leave Michelle back to her duties and head toward a soft blue carpeted hallway with walls painted in soft yellow hues.

As we walk, I hear distant barking.

"I wonder who that can be?" I say with a playful smirk.

"That's Amiga! She already hears my voice," Ignacio says. I look up at his chiseled profile which has a sexy five o'clock shadow and specks of gray. "My room is all the way at the end of the inn as to not bother any of the guests but she sometimes can't help but bark. She's a dog!" He grins which makes his eyes crinkle.

When we approach his room, I hear scratching at the door and some whimpering.

"She gets excited when she sees me." I can totally relate.

He slowly turns the brass handle and opens the white wooden door. From the slant of the doorway opening, I see a white little blur leaping and running around in circles.

"Hola Amiga! How's my little girl," Ignacio says in a baby talk.

He scoops her up in his arms like a toddler. She showers him with kisses which makes him giggle.

"I just saw you two hours ago! You're acting like I haven't seen you in days. Tommy, meet Amiga! Slowly hold out your hand so she can smell you," he instructs. I follow his directions.

Amiga sniffs me and then starts softly licking my knuckles.

"Awe, she's giving you little kisses, besitos. See, she likes you already." Her wet tongue tickles my fingers. I can't help but smile at the little dog and pet her.

Ignacio then places her back on the floor and she immediately paws at my knees. She looks up at me with little soulful brown eyes.

"Well, hello to you too! Nice to meet you, Amiga." I bend down and she puts forward her right paw.

"Shake her paw. That's her way of shaking your hand. I taught her. She is a very smart dog, right, Amiga?" Ignacio says, again beaming with pride. And as strange as it sounds and looks, I actually shake her right paw.

"Does she high-five too, Ignacio?"

He looks at her and to my surprise, she, well, gives me a high-five.

She then sprawls out on the floor where I use my fingers to brush her thick white coat. Again, she looks up at me with her deer-like eyes. Do dogs purr? I think this one does.

As I stroke the top of her head, Ignacio grabs her leash and places it on her. She knows the routine and simply follows his lead.

"Ready to take a walk with our new friend Tommy? Show him what a good girl you are, Amiga!" he continues in his baby talk.

She gently barks and I take that as a yes. I'm enjoying watching this masculine man dissolve into mush around his beloved dog. It's endearing.

As soon as we step outside his room, Amiga pulls and pulls ahead like a furry tug boat. The girl's got to go.

We pass the cheery front desk clerk again and then head outside where Amiga immediately squats and does her business on some of the pansies we passed earlier.

Amiga then leads the way back to the cliff walk where she happily sniffs at all the benches, grass and flowers. Her little black tail wags as furiously as a windshield wiper moving horizontally. As Ignacio and I continue our walk, our steps fall in sync as we stride side by side. Every now and then, Amiga looks up at me whenever I speak. She's probably thinking, *Who is this guy with the messy hair and weak hand shake? A human Chia Pet?*

At a bend in the trail, we sit down on a wooden bench where Amiga leaps onto Ignacio's lap, wiggles her butt and makes herself comfortable.

"This is our favorite spot. I mean, look at the views," he says, pointing to a passing ship in the distance.

The darkness of the ocean blurs with the night sky which is sequined with twinkling stars. The breeze is stronger from earlier, now lifting Amiga's white fur. The lights from the town only illuminate the immediate part of the shore.

To my left, I see the neck of the beach where the window lights of Huckleberry's restaurant and the Neptune Motor Inn dot the length of Beach Street like a collection of holiday lights. Since there aren't any tall buildings here, it feels like you can peer endlessly into the night from all directions.

"This is why I love living here, Ignacio. You can't beat this view or breeze," I say, the wind tickling my face.

"Hey, did you see that, Tommy?" Ignacio says, pointing ahead of me. "It's a shooting star. Go ahead, make a wish."

I turn to him and smile. His eyes twinkle like two stars.

"Okay, I just did. Did you, Ignacio?"

"Mine already came true," he says with a shy grin.

As he looks at me with his tender eyes, my cheeks suddenly warm. I don't know what to say.

"And what did you wish for, Ignacio?"

He leans into my ear and whispers, "That I would get to see you again and here we are."

"What did you wish, for Tommy?" he says, slowly pulling back.

"Can I tell you on our second date? I don't want to jinx it or anything but it's a good wish. I promise."

"So we are having a second date?" Ignacio says with a big grin and raised eyebrows.

"If we do, then part of my wish comes true. It's a two-part wish," I say, turning ahead and looking again at the performance of stars before us. I'm embarrassed to admit how much I like this guy. He's so easy to talk to and be with.

"Are the stars like this in Costa Rica?"

"They are bigger, brighter and more beautiful, if you can believe that. From San Jose, you see the stars hang right above the mountains. I used to lay in my parent's pool and tried to count them. There's nothing quite like the view of the mountains there," he says with a faraway look. But I'm enjoying the view of him.

"Do you miss your family in Costa Rica? Maine is a *looong* way from them and your rain forest paradise."

My index finger slowly outlines Ignacio's sun tattoo on his wrist. My right foot lazily swings against his left foot. I like this scene. It's intimate, sweet, natural.

"I talk to them once a week. And I go down for the holidays and spend a week or so during each trip. I see my little nephews and nieces. I love them dearly but I also like my privacy and space," he says.

"Um, do they know that you're, you know, gay?"

Ignacio turns to me and purses his lips.

"They do and they don't. I don't discuss it with them but I'm in my mid40s, single and living with a pretty dog named Amiga and running an inn in an artsy town. I think that gives it away."

"And your hair relaxer!" I tease. "Just kidding. Your hair looks naturally wavy and thick."

Ignacio's facial expression softens again but with animated eyes.

"Amiga, did Tommy Perez just say that I'm super gay?"

Amiga barks in agreement. I also playfully woof woof back.

"I think the tribe has spoken, Ignacio! Seriously, I wouldn't have guessed you were gay if I hadn't seen you at the bar that night. You're not just handsome but masculine too," I say, surprising myself for being so forward again. I blame it on the drinks.

For the record, I had two but I am still feeling buzz-happy. When I'm around Ignacio, I feel like I'm wrapped up inside a bubble of giddiness and joy where time seems to run at a difference pace. I don't know why or what it is because I can't remember the last time I felt this way. Is it just a friendship, lust or more?

"Well I knew you were gay because of your hair!" he says with a flirty smile.

"My hair? What's gay about it?" I say, plastering it down again with my hand and feigning offense.

"The way you were twirling it at the bar as you sipped your drink! That's what caught my attention. You don't meet many guys in Maine with hair like yours. Most men here have a buzz cut or short cropped hair. Your curly hair reminded me of the guys in Miami, Brazil or Greece. I thought it was cute. I still do," he says, brushing his shoulder up to mine.

"Why, thank you, I think?" I look at him side eyed with narrowed eyebrows.

"So what are your plans for the weekend, Mr. Tommy Perez?"

I tell him that I actually have to work tomorrow. Bummer.

"I have to interview a local writer. It's a follow up story. He's not just big in Maine. He's national too!" I say, now playing with the tips of Amiga's ears. They're big and sort of remind me of Gizmo, the cute fuzzy Gremlin from that 1980s movie.

"Who is the writer?" Ignacio asks.

"Richard Blanco. You know, the inaugural poet for President Obama from a few years ago. He is releasing a new edition of his memoir and he has a reading tomorrow in Portland. I'm interviewing him before the reading for a news feature. My friend Carlos is driving up for the event because he's a big fan of his poetry. It's the whole gay Cuban thing, you know. Carlos and I joke around that his name translates into Dick White."

I laugh at my silly inside joke with my fellow amigo.

"If you're not doing anything, maybe you could drop by the reading and say Hi. We'll be there. We can have dinner or drinks after in Portland."

"Sounds good to me, Tommy. I've heard of Richard Blanco. I'm curious to hear him read. But to be honest, I'm more interested in seeing you again. I want to make that second wish come true," Ignacio says, slowly placing his arm behind the back of the bench where I sit.

As he moves closer, I catch a whiff of his masculine citrusy cologne and the clean smell of his Polo shirt. A tingle rushes through me.

"Me too. Having you there will be a treat!"

And as soon as I say treat, Amiga's ears perk up like two letter As. She suddenly climbs on top of me and starts licking my chin. I giggle as I try to dodge her advances.

"Oh my God, what is she doing, Ignacio?"

"You said her favorite word, Tommy. TREAT! Now you have to give her one," he says, pulling out a small bone-shaped biscuit from his pocket and handing it to me.

"Go ahead, she won't bite you. She may just lick you to death until you give her the treat."

I take the treat from Ignacio and give it to Amiga. She bites off a piece from my hand as if it were the last piece of a food in the entire world. She makes loud crunching sounds as she chews the little biscuit on my lap.

"See, I told you she would like you," Ignacio says, with a sweet grin. He then casually places his hand behind my head and softly rubs the back of my hair. I squirm in delight. Once again, a wave of tingles sweeps over me. I lean my head back into Ignacio's hand. This all feels so natural, so nice, so *good*. Pangs of happiness strike me like arrows dipped in the sweetest honey.

I look over at Ignacio and gaze into those tender olive eyes again.

"Um, can I have a treat?" I say softly.

He smiles, leans over and plants a wet sensuous kiss on my lips.

And the rest of my wish comes true.

7

NOTEPAD AND DIGITAL recorder in hand, I walk up the front steps of the Merrill Auditorium on Myrtle Street in downtown Portland. It's late Saturday afternoon, the sunlight reflects on the center's doors as I open them. Tacked on one of the doors is a big flier with Richard Blanco's toothy grin announcing tonight's event.

Once inside, I spot Richard Blanco sitting in a chair reading some notes from a book and notebook. Some theater workers vacuum, wipe down some of the glass window displays and attend to the restrooms in the empty theater. Upon hearing the door close, Richard looks up in my direction and smiles with his dimpled chin. He waves and begins to walk over in his tight-fitting gray dress shirt, blue slacks and black shoes. His salt and peppered hair is perfectly combed back except for the part that spikes up in middle.

"Hola! You must be Tommy Perez, from *People,* right?" he says, with a handshake followed by a strong hug that seems to swallow my thin frame.

"Yeah, that's me!" I squeak out, my nose tickled by his wet hair gel and strong masculine cologne. My notepad pats his upper back.

"It's very nice to meet you, Tommy Perez."

"Same here, Richard. Is this still a good time for the interview? It shouldn't take more than 20 minutes or so, " I say, visually appraising the hunky poet. With his chiseled features, he looks more handsome in person than on TV or from the back of his book jackets.

"Perfect time! We have the place to ourselves for the next half hour or so feel free to ask away. I'm literally an open book," he says, smiling and holding up his book. I grin at his humor.

I follow him inside the grand auditorium which reminds of a classic church or cathedral with its soft lighting and wood-paneled facade. We pass rows of plush red chairs that I'm sure will fill up with all his book fans, including Carlos whenever he gets here. (He runs on Cuban time, always arriving late to events by half hour or so because my loco friend gets lost easily.) As Richard and I walk, I glance back at the rest of the theater, with its rows of curved balconies that look infinite. And I wonder, what must it be like to be a best selling author, to be able to fill up so many seats?

When we reach the steps by the side of the stage, Richard gestures for me to follow him. He then squats down by the lip of the stage, his legs boyishly dangle over the edge. He pats a spot next to him, suggesting that I sit there and so I bend down and scoot over. It's just us facing this empty hall, the bright lights in the top tier makes me squint a little. Besides our voices, the only other sounds come from the electronic hums of the air conditioner above us.

I click on my recorder to start the interview, which will be a short Q and A for the back of the magazine. Usually these interviews are done by phone but my editors suggested that I drive up to Portland since it's not even an hour from Ogunquit. They also thought having fresh photos of him at the event would add to the story so a photographer should be arriving soon.

"You've always written poetry. Why take on a memoir, with long chapters?" I turn to Richard. He looks up and pauses for a moment before answering in his raspy Miami-Cuban accent.

"It was more out of creative curiosity. Every genre has its limitations. Poetry delves into the emotional core. While it's my calling, I felt there was so much to unpack from my poetry. With prose, it's about character, I can get more into the storytelling and not feel so confined to a stanza. I just wanted to write in long form," he says, eyes crinkling.

"Why call it The Prince of Los Cocuyos?"

"That's prince of the fireflies. In the book, I talk about how I worked at my family's bodega stocking shelves and learning to be a man. It was called El Cocuyito or little firefly. I felt like a little prince there at the store during those summers and the store is a character in itself in the book because so much of my realizations about being gay happened there in my teens."

"How has your recent celebrity affected your personal life?"

"Well, I'm definitely more recognized especially here in Maine and Miami. I still live in Bethel with my partner of many years. In that sense, things are still the same. I just travel more. I feel like I live at the Delta airport terminal." He grins which causes a deep dimple in his left cheek.

"Do you see yourself getting married?"

To that question, Richard Blanco unleashes a devilish grin, rolls his eyes and continues speaking in his slight effeminate voice.

"Why... are your proposing or something, Tommy Perez? " I glance down at my notepad, shake my head and laugh.

"Um, no. Not me. But I bet our readers may want to propose to you. I think they'd be curious to know whether you might write your own wedding vows one day since same-sex marriage is legal in Maine and everywhere in the US."

"For all intensive purposes, my partner is my husband. We have a mature love. We don't make goo goo eyes at each other anymore. I think we're going to make it official soon once I am done with my tour and speaking engagements. There's a scoop for you, Tommy. Write that down in your notebook," he says tapping the top of my pad with his index finger.

"Okay, okay. I'm writing it down! Since we're on the topic, where would you want to get married?"

"Hmmm," he says, putting his index finger on his chin and dramatically looking away toward the entrance of the auditorium.

"We could always go down to city hall and keep it simple but that would be boring, no? I can imagine us having a beautiful old-fashioned ceremony in Havana, with my mom and brother there and all our friends and family. As you know, I was conceived there, born in Madrid and then imported to the United States, all within 45 days of birth so I can't think of a more romantic tropical backdrop than Cuba. The country still inspires my writing which is one of the reasons why I wrote my memoir. I wanted to bottle the Cuba that my family brought to Miami, that sense of nostalgia. I wanted to show how both places influence one another and me. I wanted to make that physical landscape of South Florida a character in the memoir. Now that I live in Maine, whenever I visit Miami, I notice a new building or a high rise. The city continues to evolve. I want people to see the way things used to be there, not for better or worse, just the way they were. So yes, I'd love to get married *en Cuba!* Especially now that it's easier to travel thanks to President Obama's easing of restrictions."

I furiously scribble away.

"And speaking of, would there be a special presidential guest to this island wedding?"

Richard Blanco unleashes his toothy grin again.

"Of course, the Obamas would be invited. Maybe Beyonce too," he says with a snap of his fingers for effect.

I follow up with a few more questions about the book (it took him a year to write after he was chosen to the President Obama's inaugural poet) and his upcoming plans (working on another memoir about coming out in Miami during his twenties). Before I know it, I've asked him all the questions I had written down earlier and my 20 minutes have come and gone like a Maine tide. I notice that some fans are arriving and beginning to take their seats ahead. Some call out to Richard and wave.

"The show will start soon, guys! Thank you for coming!" he shouts out to the early birds.

"And I think that's my cue. That does it for me," I say, turning off my recorder and placing it in the front pocket of my red and white plaid shirt.

"Perfect timing, Tommy. I think I need to go back stage and finish getting ready.

You know how us Miami men are, we like to make an entrance," he says with dramatic flair, his hands up in the air.

He gets up and then offers me a hand to pull me up. I smooth out my shirt and blue jeans.

"Oh, before I forget. My best friend Carlos is coming here and he wanted me to ask you to sign his book. Could you..."

"Of course, Tommy. When I start signing books, please come straight to the front of the line so you guys don't have to wait. I'd be more than happy to sign your friend's copy."

Richard then leans in and gives me a big hug again.

"Thank you again for taking the time to interview me. I hope you enjoy the reading. And if you see your photographer, just send him to the dressing room backstage where I'll be hanging out."

"Thanks Richard. I will. See you after the reading."

With that, he waves and recedes toward the rear of the stage. I step down to the mezzanine level and step back up the aisle toward the lobby. I want to see if I spot Carlos or Ignacio.

Just as I approach the carpeted lobby, in walks in what's becoming a familiar sight. Danny. As in the freelance photographer who keeps popping up in my life lately. This marks the third time I've run into him in the last few weeks. There must be some type of meaning to all this but what? But we do have at least one friend in common and we are in the same business. I just have to laugh at the situation.

With his breezy confident swagger, Danny strides inside the lobby. His camera gear hangs off his lean frame which is framed by a long-sleeved sky blue shirt and baggy blue jeans. He suddenly spots me. He wiggles his eyebrows and waves.

"TOMMY! BEST MAN!" he barks out loud as he approaches me. I'm instantly reminded of the way he first spoke to me at Rico's wedding.

"Present! Let me guess, you're my freelance photographer for the Richard Blanco interview," I say, leaning my head to the right and tucking my notepad into my rear jean pocket.

"Of course! I'm your friendly neighborhood photographer. We have to stop meeting like this. I might begin to think you're stalking me or something," he says with a cocky smirk.

"Um, you're the stalker! You're shooting MY ASSIGNMENTS."

"Well, your magazine editors assign THE BEST. Look at the play that you're Broga story got! It was a two page spread, thanks to my *fabulous* photos. I felt like I captured the true essence of Broga," he says, looking up and holding up his hand as if making a speech.

"I happen to think that my story had just a little something to do with that too, Danny. Besides, words trump images."

Danny feigns shock and covers his mouth with his left hand. His blue eyes are all animated, the pupils expanding like two big dots.

"I think you've got it wrong. It's the other way around. Images can succeed without the written word."

"But the words give the images context, they explain the picture," I say, mimicking taking a photo with an invisible camera.

"And some pictures don't need to be explained. They just are. They're subjective. Eye of the beholder, BEST MAN!"

My eyes narrow. My teeth start grinding. My upper back stiffens. What is it about this guy, who like a photograph is so beautiful to marvel, but then ruffles my feathers at the same time? Why does he have that effect on me? At least with Ignacio, he listens and shares in his own quiet sexy way. With Danny, it's this back-and-forth, a simmering heat.

"Well, try explaining Richard Blanco or Broga without my writing," I fire back. "Without the words, People magazine would be just photos of people. It would be called PHOTOS or SELFIES! You need the storytelling to go with the images."

"And that's what photos do," Danny says with a raised eyebrow. "For what it's worth, I think we make a good team, Tommy. Your words, my images even though my images can stand without words. I actually like your writing. You paint images with your words," he says with an ease of an old friend.

The compliment catches me off guard and I feel my cheeks warm. Flattery goes a long way, especially with writers. For all his teasing ways, Danny can be nice when he wants to. I think he's trying to smooth the conversation. And I have to agree, we do make a good team.

"Why thank you, Danny. I think you complimented me just now." I place my hand over my heart.

"So where's the man of the hour, the one and only Mr. Richard Blanco?" Danny asks, scanning the lobby.

I explain that he's backstage and that the reading should begin shortly.

"Cool! I'll grab some portraits of him now and then take some of him engaging with the crowd. I'll upload them to your editors as soon as I can. And then I'll be on my way back to Massachusetts."

"I'm all yours, uh, I mean he's all yours, Danny."

"Freudian slip, Tommy?"

"Um, no," I say, narrowing my eyes. "Just...um, never mind."

"So what's our next assignment, BEST MAN? I figure we should plan these things ahead of time if we are going to keep bumping into each other like this."

"Actually, I think our next event is a wedding. Carlos Martin's to be exact! He's going to be here for the reading. You guys can meet in person."

"That's great! We're supposed to meet in a few days but this might be better. We've already discussed some of the logistics over the phone. So if we don't run into each other on anymore assignments, we'll at least see each other next month in Key West!"

"I'm looking forward to it, I mean, the wedding. I'm Carlos's best man."

Danny and I exchange a grin. "You're like BEST MAN for hire!... Well, I'm going to go find Mr. Blanco. I'll look for you and Carlos after the reading. Maybe we can all grab some coffee or a drink in town."

"That sounds like a plan. We'll wait for you outside the theater, " I say. And then I remember that Ignacio will be here too. I can invite him along. The more, the merrier, right?

"Okay, that sounds good. See you later, BEST MAN TOMMY PEREZ!" Danny says in his loud drill-sergeant voice.

I wave and walk outside and look for my loco friend.

8

"LOCO, HE SIGNED my book! I can't believe he signed my book," Carlos gushes as we wave goodbye to Richard Blanco. A huge line of fans waits for him to sign their books. As we make a beeline toward the exit, Carlos rereads the dedication for the third time in two minutes.

"We need to hang out more in Maine, loco," Carlos says. The sun is beginning to set, transforming the sky into a swirl of pink, yellow and orange.

"We could if I can get you to drive up here more. Hint hint. It's usually me heading to Boston to see you or Rico."

"I know but Nick likes hanging out in Boston with his buddy Gabriel and it's hard to get Nick to drive on the weekends. He prefers to take the T when we go out because he doesn't like spending money on gas. I love the guy but he's a cheapo. I think his name comes from the word nickel. Anyway, I promise we'll try to visit more often especially if you have another handsome celebrity to interview. Sorry, loco."

I playfully purse my lips and give Carlos a sideways look as we walk down the steps of the auditorium. Other smiling book fans walk away, clutching their copies to their chests like high school yearbooks.

"Hey, so where's your Costa Rican friend, Tommy? Didn't you say he was coming?" Carlos turns to me.

Throughout the reading, I kept an eye out for Ignacio but didn't see him.

"I don't know. He said he'd come. Let me check my smartphone. I had it on silence during the event."

I pull out my phone and notice that there's a text message from Ignacio.

It reads, *Hi Tommy! I'm so sorry but I can't make it tonight. We have a broken water pipe in one of the rooms and I have to stay and take care of the situation. Send Mr. Blanco and your friend my greetings. Besos, Ignacio!"*

I respond, *No worries. We'll hang out again soon. Stay dry! Say Hi to Amiga for me!*

Despite my excitement of interviewing Richard Blanco and seeing my old friend, I'm feeling like a deflated balloon. I was looking forward to seeing that handsome face again. I keep picturing him kissing me on Marginal Way.

"What's wrong Tommy? Your smile is gone!" Carlos says, mimicking my smile by holding his fingers to his lips like a mime.

I hold up my phone and show him the message.

"That's too bad. Another time then. But hey, I'm still here, loco. Party of two so let's get a drink and something to eat. I didn't drive all this way for nada," Carlos says with his animated light brown eyes.

"Of course! I was just looking forward to seeing Ignacio and introducing him to you."

"And you will, Tommy."

We trek toward my VW Beetle which is parked at the end of the street when I hear -

"YO, BEST MAN! Where do you think you're going?"

I turn around and see Danny waving from the steps of the center. I totally forgot about our plans. I'm such a goof.

"Hey, isn't that my wedding photographer, Tommy?" Carlos says pointing to Danny.

"Very perceptive. I forgot to tell you that he was here shooting my Richard Blanco story. I told him we could all hang out after."

"Perfect, loco. I had plans to meet up with him in Boston next week but this is even better. We can talk some more about the wedding."

I place my arm around Carlos's shoulders and we walk back to the center.

"Loco, he's hot, more handsome than the photo on his website. How could you forget...*about that!*," he says squeezing my arm.

"Well, ahem, a certain someone kept babbling about some inaugural poet and writing notes all over my notepad during the reading and distracting me."

"Hmm, I wonder who that could be," Carlos says with a smirk while looking away at the darkening sky.

We both laugh.

As we approach Danny, he has his happy go-lucky smile which could star in its own toothpaste ad. He then quickly snaps some photos of Carlos and me as we walk and talk toward him.

I feign offense.

"Please, no paparazzi! I'm trying to keep a low profile," I joke, holding out my hand in front of my face and looking away like a Kardashian.

"It's the BEST MAN and BEST GROOM!" Danny announces like a radio broadcaster. "Don't worry, Carlos. These are on the house."

He puts down the camera and lets it hang off his shoulder. Danny then moves in to give me a hug and then Carlos.

"So nice to finally meet you in person, Carlos. Congrats again on the engagement."

"Thank you Danny! Good to meet you in person as well," Carlos says as he hugs Danny who at six-feet tall dwarfs my friend and me.

And for the hell of it, Carlos and I look at each other, hug and laugh in a silly way that only old friends can.

"Tommy, I'm all done with the assignment. Do you still want to hang out?" Danny says with a sweet grin.

"Sure, we're going down to the wharf to find a place to grab a drink and hang out. Want to drive with us? I'm parked right down the street." I point behind me.

"Yeah, come out with us, Danny. We can all get to know each other better. Right, loco?"

"Yes, Carlos." I level a straight-face expression before a smile curls on the edges of my mouth revealing my amusement.

We begin to stroll along the cracked sidewalk and pass some weathered red-bricked office buildings which all seem to look the same here.

Once we get to my car, I open the passenger door and fold the black front seat forward. Carlos climbs into the back seat, followed by Danny who rides shot gun. I loop around the car and hop into the driver's seat when I notice Carlos silently speaking to me through the rear view mirror.

"Ignacio who?" Carlos says holding up his hands and shrugging his shoulders.

I arch my eyebrows, widen my eyes and silently mouth back "Stop it, loco!"

Carlos responds with "Danny is super cute," while pointing to the back of his seat.

And then Danny turns around and looks at Carlos and then me.

"Tommy, I see your lips moving but I'm not hearing anything. Are you daydreaming or something, BEST MAN!"

I look down and start grinning. I then notice Carlos covering his mouth and quietly laughing to himself in the rear view mirror.

"Sorry about that. I was just thinking about something. I didn't mean to be rude or anything."

"You're a strange bird, BEST MAN!" Danny says, his voice laced with curiosity as I start the engine and begin to pull away from my space.

At an old tavern in downtown Portland not far from the wharf which is filled with small and big commercial fishing boats, cawing sea gulls and homeless people looking for a handout, we sit in a wooden booth by a window. Danny sits to my right and Carlos across from us. We order drinks from the pasty-faced, Goth-looking waitress who looks about twenty-something. I get my usual. Carlos orders a rum and Coke (also known as a Cuba Libre) and Danny just asks for a club soda with ice which I find odd because you usually mix that with something else.

As we wait for our drinks, Danny and Carlos naturally talk about the wedding in Key West. Every now and then, I find myself staring out the window and looking at the mix of locals and tourists walking up and down the cobble-stoned inclined street thick with shops, boutiques, and bookstores.

"Carlos, so what's the theme of your wedding? I know it's in Key West but that's just the backdrop."

Carlos's eyes light up as they usually do when he talks about Nick and their upcoming nuptials. He fingers his engagement ring as he speaks.

"Bueno, it's a Cuban, Portuguese-Irish wedding to celebrate both our families. Obviously, my side is the Cuban part and Nick's family is a mix of Portuguese and Irish. I know it sounds like a big mishmash but it'll work. It's us! We are going to exchange vows in English. But I am also using some words in Spanish and some in Portuguese to acknowledge our families. And Tommy here," Carlos says tapping the top of my right hand to make sure that I am paying attention even though I was looking at a hot guy walking down the street, "will recite a poem about Nick and me and how we met. Right, loco?"

"Of course! I already started writing it. The poem will rhyme too and it well tell your story. But be warned, I'm not a poet. I'm a journalist but I promise you that it will flow, bro. See, I'm already rhyming."

Danny grins at me in a devilish way. He seizes the opportunity to jump in.

"BEST MAN is a poet? No way. Like, there-once-was-a-man-from -Nantucket-type of poet?"

I turn to him and knit my eyebrows.

"Um, no, not like that. Please. Give me some credit. I'm more of the roses-are-reds-and-violets-are-blues kind of poet. Just kidding. I'm treating this like a story but a very personal one that happens to rhyme. Hey, it's not as easy as it sounds. Try finding a word that rhymes with Cuban or Providence, where Nick is from?"

"Cuban. Fusion. Losing. Moving," Danny rattles on.

"And Providence. Audience. Confidence. Bottomless," Danny continues, which makes me wonder where he pulled out the word bottomless from.

"Hey, those are pretty good, Danny although I would have never thought of pairing Providence with bottomless. Maybe there's a writer in you after all," I say, grabbing my smart phone to text message myself the words he just rhymed.

I then turn toward Danny and playfully take a picture of him with an imaginary camera. He playfully blocks my invisible camera the same way that I did earlier when he took photos of Carlos and me on the street.

"I'm trying to stay incognito. No cameras *por favor*. I don't want to be in some celebrity tabloid like People magazine!" Danny says in theatrical fashion.

Carlos laughs.

"Whatever my loco friend comes up with will be great. I trust him. I know he'll come through for me as he always has since I moved to Cambridge. Tommy is the man," he says with a fist bump to this chest.

The waitress returns with our drinks and carefully places each of our glasses down before dashing back to the bar. The counter is filled with yuppies and college students chatting and watching TV monitors carrying broadcasts of New England Cable News and reruns of

Big Bang Theory. Van Morrison's *Brown Eyed Girl* suddenly plays on the speakers in the background. My fingers tap to the beat on the table while underneath, my feet move to the rhythm. *My Brown Eyed Girl*...Carlos then invites us to make a toast.

"To Key West and new good friends," he says, clinking my glass and then Danny's.

"And to BEST MAN and BEST GROOM. My new amigos!" Danny says, raising his glass to each of ours.

"CHEERS!" we all announce at the same time which makes the other bar patrons turn around and look at us.

We all take a sip and smile at one another. I am liking this scene. The conversation flows easily between the three of us. Danny fits right in as he talks about his various photo assignments, how we've bumped into each other lately in unlikely places and how he's looking forward to Key West.

I'm thinking he can be a new friend to add to our little New England clique even if I find him, kind of dreamy. This, despite his annoying way of calling me BEST MAN. But that's kind of growing on me too.

"I've actually never been to Florida. I spend most of my time shooting in New England. I've traveled to the West Coast and Atlanta but not that far south," Danny says, twirling his straw between the chunks of ice in his club soda.

"Tommy can be your tour guide and show you around Cayo Hueso. That's what we call it in Spanish," Carlos says, playing the obvious cupid.

"Hey, that would be great BEST MAN! Key West as seen through a Florida native."

"It's one of my favorite places, Danny. I used to drive down there when I was a reporter in Miami. The three–hour trip relaxed me. Imagine being surrounded by different shades of blue on a thin highway and feeling a certain tropical breeze. And once you're down there, your worries seem to melt away. You have the Atlantic Ocean on one side and the Gulf on the other. There's something magical about Key West besides the colorful sunsets. The place is a state of mind."

I place my right hand under my chin and gaze out the bar window as if I were looking out at the bars and shops of Duval Street.

"Well, I'm sold. I want to capture those beautiful sunsets that I've heard so much about. I can bring my Leica camera for some personal shots, too."

"Bueno, that's why the wedding will end just before sunset. The colors! The red, purple, and pink hues. It's so romantic and so perfect for our wedding, " Carlos says. He then leans in closer to Danny.

"Speaking of weddings Danny, have you ever thought about getting married now that it's legal? Um, do you have a boyfriend?" Carlos asks as I sit there with mouth as wide as a black hole as my friend asks these super personal questions. Now who should be called loco? Carlos, that's who! He's interviewing Danny for a job opening called Tommy's-future –boyfriend even though I had begun to reserve that slot for Ignacio. My cheeks warm from embarrassment. It's official, Carlos is the new Captain Obvious, coming to a theater near you.

Danny grins at Carlos's forwardness before his eyes suddenly begin to turn...sad?

"Um, well, I did have a boyfriend three years ago. His name was Rick and I thought we'd get married one day in Massachusetts but... we...ran, um, out of time," Danny says softly, stumbling on the words. He exhales and pauses before continuing.

"Rick passed away. And I haven't really met anyone since. Work keeps me busy. It's a great distraction," he says with another long exhale.

Internally, I cringe and clench my teeth. I know Carlos didn't intend to pry into something so sensitive, so private. He was just trying to make conversation and help me get to know this cute photographer and vice versa. It was all innocent.

"I'm so sorry, Danny," I say, placing my right hand on Danny's shoulder and squeezing softly.

"Oh man! I had no idea, Danny. My condolences. You don't need to explain or anything. I'm sorry if I came off intrusive," Carlos says, looking embarrassed while extending his hand to Danny's to comfort him.

"Thanks guys. It's okay. You didn't know. I've gotten better talking about Rick in the past year or so. He was a great guy, full of life, handsome. He helped promote and raise funds for a nonprofit food pantry. He loved his job and me. He was hit by a drunk driver while riding his bike early one morning in Plymouth where his family lived. It was just one of those things that you read in the paper or see on TV and you never think it could happen to you. Well, it did. We were together for two years and we were really in love. I think that's why I enjoy photographing weddings so much because it reminds me that love is infinite and all around us. It reminds me of how I felt for Rick. True love. It gives me hope that I may find it again one day."

I look into Danny's eyes, two blue pools of sadness. They may explain why he ordered a club soda with no alcohol.

He must have noticed my sympathy and my eyes watering a little because he suddenly looks away and changes the subject.

"Anyway, BEST MAN and BEST GROOM, you guys will have to show me a good time in Margaritaville! I want to see all that Key West has to offer. "

"OF COURSE!" Carlos and I say at the same time. We look at each other and grin which lightens the mood.

"We're the Beantown Cubans!" I declare as Carlos and I high-five one another.

"And you're part of our group now!" Carlos says warmly to Danny who looks at Carlos and then at me with a smile.

"We look out for each other!" Carlos says.

9

SUNDAY MORNING FLIES by as I sit at my small wooden desk transcribing my interview with Richard Blanco. To my right, a Red Sox mug filled with pens and pencils. My desk faces a small window where the day's bright buttery sunlight pours in. I'm working again when I could be outside bike riding or running but I shouldn't complain. This is self-inflicted. I'm working today because I want to get this out of the way to make tomorrow easier for me when I start a new assignment. Proud overachiever or married to my job?

I grin as I listen to the part of the interview when Richard Blanco thought I was proposing to him. I can't use it in the story but it's a funny footnote. I play the recording, pause, type, play again and repeat the process all over again as I fill up my laptop's screen with copy. As I work, I think about how much fun I had last night with Carlos and Danny.

After our drinks at the tavern, we strolled along the Portland Harbor and marveled at the various boats docked in Casco Bay. One vessel that caught our eye is actually a long-time floating restaurant, DeMillo's On The Water. We all agreed how it would be cool and strange to have dinner on a large white-painted dinner boat that doesn't take you anywhere. The boat is permanently docked there.

Then we headed to the Cold Stone ice cream shop where we each had a small cup of ice cream. We continued our walk in downtown Portland up and down the historic sloped streets where we browsed in some shops and visited Longfellow Books, one of the two independent bookstores in the district.

Having Carlos in Portland, even if it was for a few hours, felt like old times when I lived in Boston where we would hang out by not doing anything in particular. Even washing and drying our clothes at his apartment was fun because it gave us a chance to exchange stories and advice. His presence in Portland reminded me how isolated I really am in Maine. Maybe Ignacio was right the other night about me being somewhat lonely up here. It's only when I'm reminded of what I had in Boston with Rico, Carlos and - yes even Mikey once upon a time - that these Boston blues return. Perhaps deep down, this is why I'm always working like this morning, to ward off the loneliness.

After the bookstore, I drove Danny and Carlos back to their cars which they had left by the arts center. Danny said he had to head home to Massachusetts to upload some of the shots he took of Richard Blanco. He also mentioned that he had an early assignment for today. Carlos also had to get going because he had late night plans with Nick in Cambridge. So everybody went home including moi who had the shortest drive to Ogunquit. I spent the rest of the night watching a marathon of reruns of *The Walking Dead* on AMC until I passed out on my plush red sofa. I woke up to the gurgling sounds of zombies chasing humans.

It's noon and I'm almost done with my Richard Blanco piece. I print it out and search for any missed typos. When I'm satisfied with the story, I then file it to my editor.

With that out of the way, the rest of the day is wide open. At my desk, I stretch my arms upward, look up at my white ceiling and crack my knuckles. I release a big y-a-w-n and loosen up my neck. I shut my laptop and power down. *Finis!* It's time to play.

I continue stretching my arms and arching my back (sleeping on the sofa will do that to you). I walk a few steps on my hardwood floors to my little kitchen which has a brick facade and white bar counter. I swing open the refrigerator door which is covered with magnets of pens and To-Do notes such as giving my VW an oil change. I grab a diet Coke from the drawer filled with a dozen similar shiny silver cans. I peel back the lid and hear the fizz fizz escape.

Taking a swig, I head over to my small living room (everything in my apartment is small. It's 600 square-feet) where colorful posters of Boston, Fort Lauderdale, Miami decorate the walls. I plop myself on my sofa and prop my feet on the wooden coffee table.

The midday sunlight glimmers through my vertical shades and warms the room. I look over toward my sliding glass door and study the stunning horizon over the Atlantic, how the white-tipped waves roll into the beach like a liquid blue curtain. That's what I should have on my wall – a framed photo of this serene view. Maybe I can ask Danny to take a picture for me sometime as a friendly favor.

Lazily lounging on my sofa happens to be my favorite thing to do in my apartment. Sometimes, I sit with my legs up on the arm rest and I simply absorb the view. The sounds of the wind brushing up against my glass doors also soothe me.

Sometimes, I crack open the doors just enough to allow the gentle sea breeze to Zen me out. And sometimes, I find myself doing all the above and fall into a deep sleep after a day of reporting and writing.

Just as I am about to turn on the TV and veg out, my smartphone vibrates from the kitchen counter. When I get up and grab it, there's a message from Danny. I open it and an image unfolds.

It's one of Carlos and me when we walked in downtown Portland yesterday. The photo captured the two of us looking at one another and sharing a laugh. In the shot, I'm covering my mouth with my right hand as Carlos laughs back, his profile captured.

Below the photo, a message reads *Thanks for hanging out last night, BEST MAN! I thought you and Carlos would want a copy of this. See you soon, wherever! Danny.*

I grin as I expand the photo with my thumb and index finger and save it. Immediately, I forward it to Carlos who responds with a smiling face emoji and a text *Thanks loco!*

I also share the photo on my Instagram account @tommyperez-writes and I print out a copy from my desk printer. I then tack it onto my refrigerator with one of pen-shaped magnets.

Not a bad way to start the day. I take a few steps back and smile at the photo on my fridge.

I down the rest of my soda, loudly burp from the corner of my mouth (sorry) and think about what I can be doing today. Maybe a binge session of *Wonder Woman* reruns? Or a quick hike in New Hampshire? Maybe I'll head into town for coffee and cozy up with the Sunday *New York Times* to read what other trend writers are covering?

Just as I'm about to turn on the TV again, a loud pounding thunders from my front door. This rattles me. I shuffle to the door and ask "Excuse me, who is it?"

"The police!" a deep voice responds from the other side.

"What, what, WHAT?"

I carefully crack open the door and I spot a familiar face. I roll my eyes and shake my head.

It's Rico wearing his aviator glasses and holding up his Subway discount card like a police badge.

"Open up, Mr. Perez. You've committed a serious crime!" he commands, now folding his arms to show off his big tanned biceps, one of his habits.

I smirk and tilt my head to the right.

"Oh really? And what might that be?" I say, opening the door wider.

"You've neglected hanging out with your Italian wingman! You've left your wingman in the dust. I hear you can serve five years for that," he says in a boyish tone, pretending to cry and rubbing his eyes with his knuckles.

I laugh at this silly scene and gesture for him to come in.

"Is this your indirect way of saying you've missed me?"

"Not at all, I was just fucking with you," he says, giving me a big hug and patting me on the back as he stomps inside my apartment.

"What are you doing up here?" I close the door behind me.

"I wanted to surprise you. SURPRISE!" Rico shouts throwing his hands toward me to scare me. "You always drive down to Boston so I wanted to return the gesture and see you up here. Besides, it's been ages since we hung out. I thought you were beginning to forget about little old me. I was having Tommy withdrawal."

"Well, for the record, you were on your honeymoon for a few weeks and then you went back to work and I've been working too and driving all over the place reporting. I do have a job, you know?"

"True but I hear you've seen more of Danny lately. *Hmmm.* I want some details, Tommy. *Capisce?*" Rico says, removing his sunglasses. He makes himself at home by opening my refrigerator and grabbing a bottle of water. He then plops himself on my sofa, his feet thud on my coffee table.

I sit on the blue love seat across from him and place my feet on the table as well.

"Well..." I tease him by drawing out the story.

"Yeah, Tommy?"

"And..."

"Yeah?"

"It's like...." I say, grinning and I can't help but giggle.

"Oh Tommy, just fucking spill it already! I do have to drive back to Boston at some point. I'm a married man," Rico says, pointing to his watch and then proudly displaying his wedding band.

"Okay..." I say, before Rico shoots me a playful yet annoyed look.

"Now I'm being serious. Danny and I have run into each other on some assignments including last night in Portland for an author event. I've had fun getting to know your photographer friend. He's cute, teases way too much and most of all, he's a great photographer. He's even going to photograph Carlos's wedding. The more I see or bump into Danny, the more curious I've become. But I was surprised to learn last night that he had a partner who died. Why didn't you mention that before, Rico? I thought your family and his family knew each other from way back." I lean back in the chair.

Rico takes a sip of his water, leans forward and then folds his hands. He looks serious and sad at the same time.

"Sorry, Tommy for not telling you about, Rick. You met Danny on my wedding day. We were all having so much fun. It was such a beautiful day and there wasn't a right time or way to say anything. Besides, it wasn't my place to tell you. That is part of Danny's past and if he wanted to open up about that painful time, it had to come from him. I hope you understand. I'm sure you wouldn't want me to tell people about your troubles with Mikey. You know my word is like granite."

"You're right. I totally understand. I appreciate you respecting my privacy as well as Danny's. It just came out of left field, you know. At least now I know why he's been single for so long."

"When Rick died, my parents went to the funeral. They said that Danny was a mess, as expected. They told me he threw himself on the coffin before it was carried out to the hearse. I was in Boston and had to work so I called him and sent him a sympathy card. The accident made news in New Bedford. There was an obituary about Rick. It's probably still online."

"Oh my God. How horrible, Rico. I feel so bad for him."

"Me too. It was my mom who suggested I reach out to him to be my photographer to help him out. When I called him up, he sounded like he was in a good place. He's had a steady flow of freelance work which has kept him busy and he seemed like his old self at the wedding. Actually, I thought you guys kinda clicked," Rico says, arching his eyebrows.

"Really? He kept barking at me and calling me BEST MAN. He still does."

Rico shakes his head and laughs.

"Oh Tommy Boy! That's his way of showing that he likes you. Don't take it the wrong way. He barks but he doesn't bite, unless you want him to. Woof woof!"

Rico holds up his hands like paws and sticks out his tongue like a dog.

I twist my nose at him.

"Speaking of dogs… I actually met a guy who has one."

"What? Who? How?" Rico says, now sounding like an owl or a reporter. I go on and tell him about Ignacio and little Amiga and our first date.

"Now I know why you haven't called me. You've been very busy whoring around my friend. Does he have a big dick? Have you sucked it yet?"

Rico suddenly makes slurping sounds and then pretends to have an invisible dick inside his mouth that he can move around with his hand.

"Umm. We haven't done anything beyond kissing and walking his dog," I fire back with a laugh.

"Well, does the dog have a big dick, Tommy?"

I grab one of my decorative pillows and toss it at him.

"The dog is a girl, dumb dumb! So NO!" I give him a mischievous grin.

"Oh…no…you…didn't!" Rico suddenly gets up and approaches me. He then swiftly picks me up and then wrestles me down on the sofa. I can't help but giggle.

"Who are you calling a dumb dumb?" he says, messing up my hair as I try to block him with my hands.

"If you want, I can give you the dog's number, Rico," I squeal, as I try to break free from his strong grip but then he pins me down on the sofa and smacks me in the face with a red pillow.

"I see the married life has made you less aggressive!"

After we wrestled and messed each other's hair like the immature frat boys that we are, Rico and I are heading to Perkins Cove for lunch. The small harbor of lobster shacks, cedar-shingled gift shops and art stores is one of my other places to hang out in Ogunquit. I enjoy walking along the wood dock and looking out at the old drawbridge which always seems to be in the up position.

I also like to lean against the dock's railing and watch the small collection of sailboats, fishing vessels and row boats that dot the water. I wonder if it's possible to hop scotch from one anchored boat to another since they all seem so close.

Rico and I grab an outdoor table at Barnacle Billy's to soak up the cool breeze and sunlight in the veranda. Bulbous beautiful red, purple and yellow flowers ribbon the restaurant's front and side garden that faces the street.

Butterflies flutter all around the flowers as if the winged creatures were oblivious to the steady stream of tourists and passers-by strolling along Perkins Cove Road toward the center of town.

"So how's the married life treating you, Rico? Does it feel any different now that you're legally husband and husband?"

I look at Rico over the rim of my menu. A strong breeze shakes the flowers and also ruffles the top of my bushy hair.

"It feels the fucking same, actually. Don't get me wrong. I love Oliver and everything but nothing has really changed. We live together. We're still in love.

The only difference is that now it's official, on paper. And I get to call him my husband instead of boyfriend or partner. I never liked those labels. Boyfriend sounds so fucking high schoolish and partner sounds like a business or medical associate. Husband sounds just right, perfect, Tommy!" Rico says, holding his smartphone to show me a picture of him and Oliver during one of their trips to Tuscany.

I smile as I gaze at the image of them holding hands and kissing in front of a vineyard.

"So the married life agrees with you! For a while, I didn't think you'd settle down. You were so commitment phobic a few years ago. It was all about hooking up at Club Cafe. Now look at you! You've come a long way."

"And I can come a long way, too!" Rico over shares, making a phallic slurping sound.

"And some things never change either!" I make a silly face at my friend.

We place our menus down to signal to the waiter that we're ready. The chubby middle-age guy with two studs in each ear hustles over with his pad and pen. He takes our orders. I ask for a grilled chicken sandwich and diet Coke. Rico gets a lobster salad and an iced tea.

"Gotta watch my abs!" Rico says, patting his tight stomach to the waiter who arches his left eyebrow and smirks while writing our orders.

"Don't mind my friend. He loves to talk about his body or show it off or both. We should all be so lucky, right?" I say, with gentle sarcasm.

"Well, he's definitely has a nice one," the waiter says, pursing his lips like a Kardashian or the Mona Lisa. Rico blows him a kiss.

"But you're not so bad yourself, curly! Don't you forget that. I'll be right back with your drinks, boys. Just hang tight," the waiter says, winking at me as he struts away toward the kitchen of the restaurant, which looks like a former grey clapboard house retrofitted as an eatery.

As we wait for our food, Rico continues to show me some more photos from his honeymoon. There are dozens selfies of him and Oliver in front of their hotel, on their balcony, in the vineyard, posing alongside their Fiat rental. Whatever the backdrop, they radiate happiness and love.

After viewing 300 images on Rico's smartphone, the waiter returns with our food. Perfect timing. I think Rico and Oliver spent most of their honeymoon taking selfies.

"Here you go, boys! Enjoy!" he says with a Miss America-type wave.

As we dive into our food, I hear a dog barking nearby. I look toward the wooden fence and I see the rim of Amiga's brown ears perk up as she jumps up and down. My view slowly shifts to her left and I see handsome Ignacio smiling and waving. Upon seeing him, waves of joy take over me and all I can do is smile like a 12-year-old girl with a boy crush.

"Who's that, Tommy?" Rico says shoving leaves of lettuce and spinach into his mouth.

"That's Ignacio, the guy I was telling you about earlier. The one with the dog. See!" I point toward him.

Rico turns around and waves.

"How are you doing Tommy!" Ignacio shouts from the sidewalk.

"Doing great. Having lunch with my wingman, Rico!"

Rico nods his way.

"Sorry, I didn't mean to interrupt. Amiga must have sensed you and started barking and jumping the fence. I guess she wanted to say Hi!" Ignacio holds up the little white furry dog and uses her right paw to wave. She immediately starts licking his hand.

"Awe!" I squeak like a Taylor Swift teenage fan while placing my hand on my heart. I look at Rico and tell him that I'm going to say Hi really quick.

"Go ahead. I'll be here stuffing my face."

I walk a few steps toward the partition when Amiga immediately begins to squirm in Ignacio's arms.

"See what I mean? She wanted to see you," he says, handing her over to me. I cradle Amiga like a baby. She then starts to lick my hand.

"But she barely knows me, Ignacio?" I say, playfully rubbing her stomach.

"You gave her a treat so you're her friend for life." Ignacio grins.

"Sorry about yesterday, Tommy. I had to work."

"No worries. I've had to break plans for stories. I totally get it. When work calls, we reporters run."

"How about if we hang out again this weekend, my treat!" Ignacio says, with a big smile.

The sunlight catches his hazel eyes, making them look greener, almost emerald. They can easily put me in a trance.

"That would be nice. Text me which day and time you're thinking and hopefully, I won't have to work again. Hey, I don't want to be rude but I should get back to my friend," I say, gently handing Amiga back to him.

Ignacio takes her and then places her back on the sidewalk but she keeps leaping up against the fence to see what's going on. Again, the tips of her ears rise up like mini friendly shark fins.

"No problema, Tommy. Enjoy the rest of your lunch," he says, giving me a kiss on the cheek. He then waves to Rico who does the same.

I look down and grin as I settle back into my chair.

"So…that's your dog whisperer?" Rico leans in, taking a sip of his iced tea. "I can't tell who likes you more, the guy or the dog?"

I toss a wadded piece of a napkin at Rico who laughs.

"He's handsome, Tommy. He does look older though."

"Yeah but that doesn't bother me. I think he looks mature. Maybe because we've become the older guys. We're 40. Remember when we were 29 at Club Café and thought the older guys were the ones in their 40s and 50s like the ladies from *Desperate Housewives*? Well, now we're those guys! We're the *Desperate House Fags*!"

"Shut the fuck up, Tommy! Speak for yourself. Technically, I'm 39. You're the one in your 40s," Rico chides me.

"Well, you're right on my heels, then," I say, twitching my nose at him.

"Anyway, Ignacio is 47 so he's not that much older than me."

"I know but the dude is almost 50 if you round it off. At least you and Mikey were the same age. Do you have a lot in common with El Dog Whisperer?"

"I'm still getting to know him. He likes to read my stories. He likes to read. He's sweet and sexy. And he speaks Spanish so that's about it. We get along and I'm curious to learn more about him."

"And Danny, too, right?" Rico flashes a knowing grin.

"Hey, I'm not married...yet. I like both guys. I need to explore my options. It's been so long since I met anyone decent. And now I have two prospects even though Danny is leaning toward the friendship box. I don't know. We'll see."

"Do you see Danny more as a friend because of his past with Rick?" Rico says with a solemn brow.

"Well...I think it would be hard to date someone whose previous partner, the love of his life, died. I wouldn't want to compete with the ghost of Rick. I think that memory will always hang over him. I think it's too early to say, Rico."

"Just follow your heart, silly goose whether that's Ignacio or Danny boy! I'm glad that you're opening up to the idea of dating again. I've been wanting to see you with someone again. It's been years since Mikey. Your heart is overdue. I think once you meet a guy that captures your heart the way Mikey did, you'll finally be able to let him go- for good! I think a part of you still misses him."

Rico is right. This is why I love my friend. Like Carlos, he knows and understands me so well. He tells me what I need to hear whether I like it or not.

And yes, sometimes I do think about Mikey. Maine happens to be full of brown-haired blue-eyed Ethan Hawke look-alikes so it's natural. If you searched for the words **sentimental**, **nostalgic** and **gay** on Google, my photo would probably pop up.

"So after lunch Tommy, let's hit some of the gay bars here. I may be married but I can still look." Rico wiggles his eyebrows.

"You got it! Thanks again for coming up today!"

Rico smiles as he holds up his glass of iced tea.

"Oh, by the way, can you spot me $2 for the toll back? I didn't bring enough cash."

I roll my eyes and laugh. My cheap friend never changes.

"So I guess drinks are on me, right?"

"Well…since you're offering, how can I say no?" Rico grins.

10

THE NEXT FEW days pass by in a blur of work assignments. I interviewed the Walshes, a couple in Maine who celebrated their 55th wedding anniversary. They live just outside Portland so I spent a day with them, looking over their vintage black and white photos and interviewing their three children.

Once I wrote that story, I moved onto another quick celebrity interview in Boston with Anna Kendrick who was in town for some screenings of her latest movie musical *Still Pitch Perfect*. And it just so happens that she's from Portland so I got to ask her about growing up there and how her parents drove her to auditions in New York City. And then I had to start gathering thread for an upcoming wedding preview for two male reality TV stars who are tying the knot at the Providence state house because one of the guys is from Rhode Island. Their nuptials are being filmed for a special episode on Bravo. That story will run just before their wedding in two weeks. *Whew!*

And before I know it, the weekend's already here. As soon as I get off my landline phone with the wedding planner for the reality TV couple, I shut my laptop and collapse on my bed. I don't want to write anything else all weekend. My brain is fried. I need some Tommy time.

I roll over on my bed, which is covered in patches of primary colors, and grab my smart phone from my wooden nightstand. Some silly messages pop up from Rico.

Have you sucked it yet? JK but not really. Call me later unless you're sucking it. LOL!

There's also a message from Carlos.

Loco, my wedding is a week and a half away. I can't believe it! We leave to Miami in a few days. Can't wait! Call me because I'm nervous! Okay!

And there's a message from (sigh) Ignacio.

Mr. Tommy Perez, dinner tonight? You, me and Amiga?

I roll over onto my back and thumb a message to Ignacio.

Hi! Sure, what time?

Meet me at the inn at 8 p.m. See you then guapo.

After responding to everyone, I roll onto my side and tuck my hands under my pillow. I take a little nap to rest up for tonight.

As I begin to doze off, my mind buzzes with questions. What does Ignacio have planned for me? He didn't say where we were going and what we would be eating? And how does his dog fit into all this? Is she coming with us? That could be cute but also limit our dining options.

But then I think of Ignacio's sparkling eyes, his chiseled profile, the swirl of grey and black in his short-cropped hair. Wherever we go, this will be a nice way to end the week and start the weekend.

An hour later, I yawn and stretch on my bed like a snow angel, my arms and legs flapping up and down. I get up and head to the bathroom where a pair of tired eyes stare back at me in the mirror.

I lean in closer and notice that my wrinkles are more pronounced, like thin lines in a dirt road. I playfully raise each eyebrow to see if that makes me look a little younger. Not really. If anything, I look like I am suspicious of something.

I think about what I told Rico the other day, how we're now the older guys that we often pointed out in the clubs not that long ago. When did this happen? Was it at 35, 38, or this past year when I turned

40? When did we cross that mysterious invisible border where we started out as youngish club guys and ended up as official older men?

Like a police cruiser on the interstate, time has crept up on us and pulled us over. At least I have my thick curly hair but even that is streaked with specks of grey if you look close enough which Carlos likes to do to make fun of me. Before I know it, I'll be 50 and ready for AARP discounts. Maybe then I'll be writing for *AARP* magazine instead of *People*. I throw my hands up in the air and surrender to life. I can't fight it. What else can I do but just enjoy my life and be true to who I am even if I'm – ugh - an older dude!

I peel off my T-shirt, shorts and underwear. I carefully step inside my shower. I allow the hot steaming water to cascade over me like a soothing balm. I lather and rinse and I feel refreshed and alive. I plop a dollop of conditioner into my hair and run my fingers through it and ooh and ahh as if I'm in my own private commercial. Thank God Ignacio or even Danny aren't here to witness this. I would never hear the end of it, especially from Danny. I quickly shave.

After a few minutes, I shut off the shower and dry off with my big beige towel. I spritz cologne all over my body and the cologne mixes with the water vapor that has steamed up the bathroom like a small sauna room. It's time to get ready for my date, whatever we are doing. Ignacio and Amiga, here I come!

It's 8 p.m. and I'm walking into the inn carrying a bottle of white wine in my right hand. I'm clean shaven, groomed; my hair is gelled to the side. I'm wearing a blue cotton short-sleeve shirt, blue jeans and brown boat shoes. Once I approach Ignacio's door at the end of the hallway, I take a deep breath and I suddenly smell some delicious cooked food. Maybe chicken? Rice? Or both. It reminds me of when my mom cooked for me during my visits to Miami. Then I knock on Ignacio's door. A blur of movement appears in the peep hole.

Ignacio opens the door and flashes a sweet sexy smile.

"Hola Tommy! Welcome back!" He pulls me into a tight embrace. He gently kisses me on the lips.

"Thanks Ignacio for inviting me over. What smells so good besides you? I could smell the food from down the hall." I step into his room where Amiga jumps up and down like a wind up toy. She paws at my knee and looks up at me. I pat her head and grin at this adorable creature.

"That's your dinner. I thought I would prepare a traditional Costa Rican dish for you. It's called a casada, a little bit of chicken, rice, plantains and beef."

"Doesn't that mean marry in Spanish?" I ask, making my way closer to a table for two by the window that overlooks the flowers that line the inn.

"Yes, it does because all the foods are married next to each other if that makes sense. They are placed next to one another, like couples."

"Ahhh, I see." I nod my head.

The table holds two gleaming plates, utensils and two empty wine glasses.

I hand him the bottle of wine.

"This is perfect. Thank you Tommy. Please, take a seat and make yourself comfortable."

I settle into the table and Amiga sits on the floor to my right, looking up at me with her big Puss-N-Boots saucer eyes. Ignacio then uncorks the bottle and then pours each of us a glass.

He ambles to his small kitchen area with each plate and serves us. He then settles into his chair across from me.

I immediately chow down, tasting the fresh salty white rice and sauteed chicken. I *mmm* and *mmm* with each bite which makes Ignacio laugh. Then I savor the beef.

"This is delicious. You're a great cook! I think I'm going to have to keep you around, " I tease in between bites.

"Thank you, Tommy. It's no fun preparing a dinner for one. When I get a chance, I like to share some of my cooking with someone special." The word special hangs in the air. I guess by someone he means other guys. Hmm. I'm sure he gets hit on a lot in this small town.

"So is this part of your date tradition – seduce a guy with good Costa Rican food?"

I continue in between bites while raising my eyebrows.

"Just the first part. You should see what I have for dessert." Amiga suddenly barks.

"I think she wants some too, Ignacio."

"You can give her a small piece of chicken. If you don't, she will never leave you alone tonight."

I grin as I place a small chunk of chicken in my hand. Just as I am about to give it to her, Amiga snatches it like an alligator, almost taking my fingers with her.

"You need to be careful, Tommy. She may eat you too. That dog is always hungry. She's a walking stomach."

"I see what you mean," I say, returning my attention back to my plate.

A few minutes later, after I tell Ignacio about my work adventures from the past week and he shares with me his week at the inn, our forks and knives scrape up the last bits of food from our plates. Ignacio gets up, takes my plate and his and leaves them in his small sink.

From the refrigerator, he removes two small plates holding a pair of golden wet domes draped in caramel. I immediately recognize them. Flan.

"Okay, this is not necessarily Costa Rican but I love flan. I thought you would too." Ignacio sets a plate for me.

"I love flan! It reminds me of Miami and my mom. She used to make us the sweetest flan ever. I think she would overload on the condensed milk but it literally tickled my tongue," I say, scooping up a piece of flan.

I look down and flashes of my mom, her red hair, her hazel eyes and infectious smile drift through my mind like a slide show. I easily envision her golden round flan and the joy she radiated in preparing it.

"I'm sorry, Tommy. I didn't mean to remind you of your mom. I'm sure she was a great cook. I'm sure she was a great lady. She made you after all."

Ignacio extends his right hand and squeezes mine. His eyes brim with pure kindness.

"Thanks Ignacio. It's okay. I think about her every day. It's been two years since she died. Pancreatic Cancer. The same thing happened to Carlos's mom in Miami but in her case it was colon cancer," I say staring down at my plate.

"I'm sorry, I really don't like to talk about my mom too much. It breaks my heart when I do, Ignacio."

My eyes begin to mist a little as I take another sliver of flan with my spoon. I do my best to push the tears back.

"Whenever you want to tell me about her, I'm here for you," Ignacio says with a warm grin.

Amiga then suddenly leaps onto my lap and starts kissing my chin.

"Awe, thank you Amiga," I say in between laughs.

"See, she sensed you were sad. She's giving you besitos, Tommy. She wants you to be happy. Okay Amiga, that's enough kisses. Let Tommy finish his dessert."

And just like that, Amiga climbs down and sits on my feet, her little body warming my boat shoes. Her kisses and Ignacio's dinner have warmed my heart tonight. I do my best to memorize all the details of this perfect night.

After dessert, Ignacio pours us some more wine. As he gathers our plates and heads over to the sink, I get up and stand by the window where I look at the bright green garden that fronts the inn. There's steady foot traffic of people walking to and from town center. Traffic is bumper to bumper as the sun begins to set in a swirl of purple and pink.

"So what do we now, Ignacio?"

"This," he says from behind, kissing the nape of my neck and wrapping me in his arms.

"That's what I was thinking, too." I close my eyes and surrender to his touch.

Ignacio's tongue slowly moves up and down the right side of my neck. I let myself lean back into his strong frame. He then gently turns me around toward him. And we're face to face. My brown eyes lock onto his hazel eyes.

"Thank you again for dinner," I say, still gazing into his eyes.

He smiles in his special sexy way which makes his eyes crinkle. He closes his eyes and kisses me deeply. I close my eyes too, losing myself in the wet soothing kisses. The warm stubble on his chin tickles mine as I rub the back of his head with my fingers. I place my glass down so my hands can run up and down the planes of his muscular back. I pull him closer. I start to kiss his neck and work my way down, slowly unbuttoning his shirt with my fingers.

My lips and fingers touch his fine black chest hairs as I peel off his shirt. I pleasure in rubbing my hands all over his smooth hairy chest like a canvas and I tickle his pink nipples which harden.

Ignacio takes my hand and leads me to his bed where he gently sits me down and pushes my body back against the cushy mattress. I scoot back to make myself more comfortable and he follows, climbing on top of me so our eyes face one another's.

I take a big gulp of air. I close my eyes as he showers me with dozens of tingle-inducing kisses all over my face and neck. I clench my fists. My body writhes with excitement. His fingers graze my arms, unleashing a sexual current that electrifies my body. I throw my arms behind my head and relish his every his touch. As we explore each other's bodies like two lost souls who have rediscovered one another, I can't help but think how right and natural this feels.

Amiga barks from her little bed in the corner and I take that she agrees with me too.

Why is my nose wet? What is touching my nose?

"Ignacio, is that you?" I say, my eyes closed.

I don't get a response besides more nose licking. I open my eyes and I see a little tongue attached to a white little furry body. It's Amiga, of course.

"I'm up, I'm up. Good morning to you!" I say between giggles which makes this little dog lick me more.

"Alright, alright!" I look to my right and notice that Ignacio is gone. I wonder where he went.

It's just me here laying shirtless in my white underwear with the dog's paws resting on my chest. I yawn and stretch my arms and legs. I turn onto my side and there's a note on his pillow.

It reads *Good morning guapo! I had to take care of an issue with the roof this morning. Enjoy your breakfast. Thank you for the great night! Talk to you later.*

Breakfast?

I prop myself up on the bed and I smell some succulent pancakes and toast which makes my stomach grumble. My eyes dart around the room to pinpoint their source. My eyes zero in on a tray above the refrigerator. He probably put it up there so Amiga couldn't reach it.

My stomach grumbles so more. I'm famished and it probably has to do with the great sexual workout I had last night with Ignacio. I smile to myself.

I climb out of bed and stretch my arms and loudly groan. I catch my reflection in a mirror by the closet. My hair looks all puffy, strands going in different directions. Tommy Bed head. I pick up my shirt from the side of the bed and slip it on. Like a shadow, Amiga follows my every move. She whines when she sees me grab the tray and place it on the table.

"Sorry Amiga. This breakfast has my name on it." She whimpers.

I dive into the stacks of pancakes, savoring every bite. With a knife, I smear syrup all over the top while I shove some crunchy wheat toast into my mouth. As I eat, I study Ignacio's room. A wall by the window features some framed photos of him with Amiga and some photos with a younger woman and a little boy and a girl. That must be his sister, nephew and niece. They're all hugging Ignacio who stands between them in front of a villa in a tropical setting.

There's another framed photo with two older people with their arms looped around Ignacio. That must be his parents by the way they each lean their heads on his shoulders. Ignacio is a clone of his father who looks about 65 with white short buzzed hair.

As I finish chowing down my breakfast, I place the plate and tray into the small kitchen sink. I amble toward the bathroom and try to fix my messy hair. Looking for toothpaste or mouthwash for my morning Godzilla breath, I open his medicine cabinet.

My eyes immediately land on three orange see-through pill bottles. Hmm. But then I close the cabinet door. This is Ignacio's business. I shouldn't be all nosy like a celebrity magazine reporter even though I am a nosy celebrity magazine writer.

I scratch my head and walk away and head back to the bed, convincing myself not to look at the names of the medications. I catch Amiga studying me.

"Don't judge! I didn't look, Amiga. I swear." She pivots her head to discern what I'm saying.

To distract myself of what could be inside those pill bottles, I decide to take an overdue shower. I peel off my shirt and underwear. I leave them on the small blue bathroom rug as I step into the tub. I turn on the shower faucet and feel the hot water cascade all over my body.

As I lather, I think of the incredible sex I had with Ignacio, the way he strummed my body with his fingers and tongue. The way he carefully kissed me from my forehead to my toes. The way he tickled my nipples with the tips of his fingers. The collection of sexy freckles that dot his upper back. The tattoo of the sun on his hairy wrist. I'm popping a boner as the night comes back to me.

But then my thoughts turn to the pills. I saw three orange bottles. If he didn't want me to see them, he would have hidden them, right?

I was honestly looking for something to freshen up my breath. But now the reporter inside me won't... let... this...go! The suspense builds up inside me like a cresting dam and I need to release it. I turn off the shower, grab a towel and step onto the mat to dry myself.

As I wrap the towel around my waist, I catch my reflection in the medicine cabinet's mirror. I can't help it. I cave in. I open the cabinet door again and remove the bottles and read their tiny labels. I'm surprised by what they're for.

One says Lexapro. Another says Paxil. The third is for acne medication. They all have active refills which means he uses them often.

From watching the TV commercials and reading stories online, I know that the first two are typically used for anxiety or depression.

But why does Ignacio take them? And what may have happened to him? I know a little about them because I considered taking something similar after my mom died but I found that writing in my journal, running and hiking helped ease the initial sadness, somewhat.

It's a feeling that will never ever really go away. You learn to live with the loss, accept it and learn to stay busy. I know that these medications while helping bring a certain stillness and calmness to the mind can also sometimes mute any creativity, at least from what I've read about them online. I didn't want them to impact my day-to-day writing so I chose my own alternatives.

As my mind wanders about Ignacio, I carefully return the bottles back to their proper places in the cabinet. I finish drying off and rub my wet hair with the edge of the towel. I can't come out and ask Ignacio about the pills. I wouldn't want him to think I was snooping around even though I was. But maybe Carlos can help me figure out this mystery and how to get Ignacio to open up about his depression or anxiety or whatever he is dealing with.

Just as I slip my underwear on and my shirt, Ignacio suddenly walks into the room. Amiga charges toward him, her ears perks up.

"There's my good little girl," he says in his baby voice as the dog jumps up and down.

As he bends down to pet her, he looks my way.

"And there's my handsome friend Tommy Perez! Did you guys have fun while I was working?" He rubs the tips of her ears.

"Yeah! We were just pilling, um I mean, chilling. Thank you Ignacio, " I say trying to cover my word vomit while putting on my pants.

Ignacio then gets up, walks toward me and plops a sweet kiss on my lips.

"Well, my home is your home. You can come here whenever you want, Tommy and you won't get charged." He grins.

"As long as breakfast is included," I tease.

"What are your plans for the rest of the day or the weekend?" Ignacio asks, rubbing the back of my head with his hand which makes me want to purr like a kitty.

"Carlos's wedding is a few days away and I need to get my suit dry cleaned and pick up a few things for the trip. Just a few errands and I need to tie up a few loose ends for some stories that I've been working on."

"Well, let's hang out before you leave for your trip. It sounds like we won't be seeing each for a few days. Amiga is going to miss you."

Ignacio scoops up the dog in his arms and points her face toward me. The dog stares back at me with those big trance-like eyes.

I tilt my head, smile and pet her.

"I think Amiga and her father will be just fine for a few days without little old me around." Despite the discovery of the pills, I know I am going to miss him too.

11

AFTER DROPPING OFF my suit at the dry cleaners and picking up some toiletries from CVS on Post Road in Wells, I stroll into Dunkin' Donuts where the succulent aroma of hot coffee greets me like the warmth of an old friend. I order an iced caramel coffee to wake me up for the rest of the day.

With my drink in hand, I walk over to a corner table of the pink and orange coffee shop where the Saturday sun beams through the window shades, warming my skin. I dial Carlos and he answers on the second ring.

"Loco! Happy Saturday! What's up?" he says. In the background, some Pitbull song plays with the familiar boom-boom-boom beat followed by his Mr. Worldwide catchphrase. I also hear the buzz of a blender in Carlos's apartment.

"Hey Carlos! I'm good. Do you have a sec? I wanted to talk to you about something."

"Of course. I'm making a blueberry-banana smoothie. I need to stay trim for the wedding. Que pasa?"

I tell him about the great dinner date with Ignacio, the hot sex, the surprise breakfast, the pills.

"What do you think he takes them for? Is there something wrong with him? Should I be worried?" I ask, twirling the pink straw in my creamy-looking drink. A couple of customers zip in and out of the shop with their plastic cups of coffee and white boxes of doughnuts.

Carlos takes a deep breath and sighs. The blender winds down. Pitbull takes a break.

"Ay Tommy. There's nothing wrong with taking anti-anxiety pills for depression. Everyone is on something these days. Sometimes, we need a little something something to take the edge off from daily life. After my mom died, I took some anti-depressants to help me get through the process. They really made a difference for a few months especially in the mornings when I felt really down and didn't want to get out of bed and go to work. The pills gave me a lift, a chemical boost. And talking to your friend Dr. Bella Solis every few weeks also helped. After a while, I began feeling like my old self and I slowly weaned off the pills. Who knows why Ignacio is taking them? Maybe he has a chemical imbalance and the meds help level him out? Maybe something tragic happened to him in Costa Rica? I don't know. Here's an idea, why don't you just ask him, loco?"

I lean back in my chair, stretch my legs and look up at the tiled ceiling.

"He hasn't brought it up and I don't know how to bring it up. It seems like a really personal thing to ask. I mean, do I just come out say 'Hey, I found some pills in your medicine cabinet. What are they for?' "

"That's one way to do it! If not, why don't you talk about me and casually mention that after my mom died, I took some pills and they helped and that you're so happy to see me getting married and enjoying life after I went through such a difficult time with my mom's loss and moving to Boston. Maybe he will talk about his depression or anxiety. Or maybe, you can talk about how someone you're writing a story about mentioned how much anti-depressants worked for them? You're good with words, Tommy. Just be yourself. If you show you care, he'll eventually open up about it."

"You're so *smaht,* Carlos," I say with a bad Boston accent.

"I know, loco. That's why dad calls me son, because I'm so bright," Carlos says, adding a drum roll sound for comic effect.

"Ugh, cheesy joke. Now you're sounding like me."

"Loco, I don't think anyone can top you in the cheesy department. You're the king of bad puns, no, make that the queen of bad puns but I love you anyway, chico."

I feign offense.

"And I love you too! You gave me another idea though. *La doctora* Bella Solis! It's been a while since I've spoken to her. I think the last time was over a year ago when I wrote a feature about her latest self-help book. It won't hurt to reach out to her and get some more advice about this. But I need to talk Ignacio first and find out why he's taking the medications. Knowing Dr. Bella, the first thing she would probably suggest would be for me to ask Ignacio sincerely about why he's on the pills, to talk to him from a place of concern and care."

"Well, it sounds like you've got a plan, Tommy. Let me know how things go with Ignacio."

"Of course! I think I'm going to finish up running errands and head back home. Speaking of errands, are you all set for the big day in Key West?"

"Almost. Nick and I leave on Wednesday to Miami to hang out with my family. Then we'll drive down to the Keys Thursday for some last minute decorations and we'll meet you there with Danny. You have the rings, right, loco?"

"Rings, what rings?"

"The one I'm going to put around your neck if you're not joking. The wedding bands! We can't have the ceremony without them."

"Oh, those! Of course I have them at home in a safe place. Don't worry."

Carlos exhales loudly.

"Whew, don't forget them!"

"I won't. Thanks again for the pep talk."

"Any time, loco. By the way, Ignacio sounds like he really likes you. The doggie too."

"Yeah, they're kind of growing on me. Enjoy your smoothie and Pitbull." I grin as I press "END" on my smart phone.

Later that afternoon, I walk into my apartment with my CVS bag in hand. I slurp the last bits of iced coffee. After putting everything away in my handy black travel bag, I head to my desk where I crank up my laptop. I look up Dr. Bella's schedule of events. Her radio show and book tours drag her all over the country so you never know where she is on any given week.

When I look up the dates for the rest of the week, I smile when I notice that she has a book signing in Coral Gables. Perfect! It would be great to see her before I drive down to Key West. She is an absolute calm. Being around her, one can't help but feel positive too which is why thousands of fans call into her radio show every day, to catch her feel-good vibe.

When I wrote my two profiles on her, one for *The Boston Daily* and the other for the magazine last year, I felt all Zenned-out as if her spiritual energy reached out and hugged me like a warm blanket. I'm hoping I'll have more details from Ignacio before my trip and perhaps share with her whatever he tells me. I dispatch an email telling Dr. Bella that I'll be in town during her book reading and that I would like to stop by and say Hi. I also leave my cell phone number.

A few minutes later after poking around my social media accounts for any new updates, my computer pings, alerting me of new email. I open it up and see that it's a message from *la doctora* herself.

Dear Tommy, it's so good to hear from you. How are you doing in Maine? I see your stories in People every week. I'm so proud of you, Tommy. Yes, I would love to see you at my book reading. I will make time for you after the reading, to discuss whatever you like. We can have tea or a late lunch at the bookstore's cafe. It's up to you. I want to hear about all the good things happening in your life. See you in Miami! Love, your doctora Bella. P.S. Remember that you have the power to change.

The email ends with her signature catchphrase which she uses to open and close each of her shows. The phrase became more of a mantra as I prepared for my move to Maine. After my second break up with Mikey, I wanted to reset my life. I wanted a new beginning in a cozy place that could also serve as a balm to my heart which was emotionally shipwrecked and stuck in Boston. I imagined leaving the stinging pain of my heart in my rear view mirror as I crossed the state line into New Hampshire and then Maine where a new optimism lay ahead. Goodbye Boston and Mikey. Hello Ogunquit. During that drive, I repeated, *You have the power to change, Tommy.* And it worked. I changed and everything in my life did too.

With the rest of the afternoon before me, I attempt watching some local TV, which mostly consists of recycled weekend news stories from earlier on New England Cable News. I channel surf while laying on my sofa with my feet propped up.

I place my hands behind my neck and my thoughts drift to Ignacio, his hairy lean and hard body. The warmth of his breath on my neck. The sweet note and breakfast he left for me earlier. But then my flashback is interrupted by some scratching sounds at the front door. Huh? Oh my, I hope it's not a raccoon or worse, a skunk. Whatever it is, its claws sound sharp, menacing.

I spring off the sofa and hustle to the front door. I slowly open it and I see the cause of the loud ruckus. A white fur ball known as Amiga. She immediately leaps toward my knees, tries to climb up and whines.

"We were walking and saw your Beetle parked outside. We wanted to say hi so Hi Tommy!" Ignacio says, firmly holding Amiga's leash. "I hope we're not bothering you or anything."

I grin as I squat down and tickle Amiga's ears with my fingers.

"Not at all, I was just scratching, I mean watching TV. As usual, there's nothing on. Come on in." I open the door wider to let them pass. Ignacio then kisses me and embraces me in a tight hug.

"Well, it's a good thing I have the only orange Beetle in town because if not, you could have ended up at somebody else's house."

Ignacio laughs as he unsnaps Amiga's leash. Like a greyhound, she charges off into the living room.

"We knew we had the right place. I mean, how many Volkswagens here have a license plate that reads QBAN."

"Oops, I forgot about that!"

I give Ignacio the grand tour of my unit which takes about ten seconds. Like a white cotton ball on a big red backdrop, Amiga makes herself at home on my sofa while Ignacio and I step inside my bedroom.

"So this is where the magic happens, where you write your stories," he says, looking around my room, which has my bed, a night stand and a desk facing the windows. In the corner, used notepads overflow in a box.

"Yep, this is the magazine's New England bureau! Impressive, huh?"

I tap the top of my laptop which sits between a bottle of hand sanitizer and my yellow note pad. Ignacio smiles as he studies the framed photographs just above my desk on the window sill. There's a photo of Carlos and me standing with our arms wrapped around each other outside our old hangout, El Oriental restaurant in Jamaica Plain.

There's another picture with Rico and me sitting on top of my old Jeep Wrangler with the top down in Provincetown. There's also a photo of me with my mom laughing as we posed in front of my newly planted yellow pansies in front of my former Dorchester brick building.

"Ah, how sweet. This must be your mom, Tommy. You have the same beautiful smile," Ignacio says with a sweet grin as he holds the framed photo in his hands. As he places it back on the window sill, his eyes pause on my yellow notepad below. He holds it up for a closer look.

"Tommy, are you researching anti-depressants?" My eyes widen. My eyebrows arch. Oh shit!

I mentally summon any answer that will sound plausible. I totally forgot that earlier, I had scribbled the names of Ignacio's medications on my notepad so I wouldn't forget them when I spoke to Carlos. I hope my face doesn't reveal the burning red shades of embarrassment I'm feeling right now.

"Oh, those are my notes. Sometimes when I talk on the phone for a story or with friends, I jot things down. It's a habit," I say nonchalantly. I think he bought my story which is half true, sort of.

Ignacio looks at me intently with his olive-green eyes and tilts his head to the side. His eyebrows narrow as if he's trying to piece something together.

"I write about all sorts of people and things. I didn't know what they were so I was going to look them up. Actually, I was going to ask Carlos if he was familiar with them because he used to take anti-depressants. Do you know anything about them?" I say, shoving myself through this window of opportunity.

I curl my toes to release some of my inner tension from this awkward situation. Amiga suddenly appears in the bedroom doorway, most likely sensing that energy in the room is off.

"Yes, I do know about them, Tommy. I happen to take these," Ignacio says neutrally.

"Oh wow. Really? What for? I'm sorry. You don't have to answer that. Now I'm being nosy. That's not any of my business. Sometimes I forget to take off my news hat. Sometimes I forget my manners. Sometimes I ..."

"It's okay, Tommy," he gently interrupts me, giving me a reassuring smile.

"I don't mind telling you. I was going to tell you anyway but, ahem, I think you beat me to the punch here," he says, cocking his right eyebrow.

I glance away and purse my lips. Guilty as charged. Busted! He probably knows I saw the pills in his bathroom.

Ignacio takes my right hand and leads me to the edge of my bed where we sit side by side. My hand holds his and squeezes in consolation. I sense he is going to share something deeply personal with me. Amiga gingerly walks toward us and sits at the foot of my bed by our feet. She looks up at us. Maybe she knows what Ignacio is about to say.

He then draws a deep breath.

"I know I haven't known you that long but I feel I can trust you with this, Mr. Perez."

"Now you're making me sound old. Sorry, I interrupted you. Go ahead," I say leaning against him, trying to keep things light.

"It's a long story, Tommy."

"I like long stories," I say with a soft smile.

Ignacio tries to hide a grin but the edges of his lips curl up. He then swallows hard and begins to tell me his story.

12

"**WHEN I WAS** younger, I had a best friend. Her name was Gwendolyn. We were inseparable in Costa Rica, going back to when we were kids," Ignacio begins, a smile escaping as he describes his friend.

As he talks, his shoulders begin to sink. His voice softens.

"She was bigger than life, Tommy! She had this beautiful spirit, this fun wild uncontainable energy, you know, the total opposite of me. Everything was an adventure with her whether we surfed, hiked, went to the movies. To her, life had no limits. It was meant to be lived. For her 16th birthday, she made me jump out of a plane with her. Oh my God! My heart races when I think about that day. I was petrified at first but being around her, I knew it would be okay, just another of many wild experiences for us to look back on when we're old and gray. Our families knew each other's and we would go on trips with them around the country and to Miami. With Gwendolyn, I felt I could tell her anything. She was the first person I told that I was gay. Of course, she knew all along. She would say to me, 'you're the sister I always wanted but you happen to have a dick.' She always kept my secret about being gay and she sometimes pretended to flirt with me in front of my family, just to throw them off. We were each other's prom dates at our high school which was an American school.

Gwendolyn being Gwendolyn, she bought me a corsage and enjoyed pinning it on my me," he says, laughing back at the memory.

"She sounds like a lot of fun, Ignacio."

"She really was. I think about her a lot."

"So where is she now? Is she still in Costa Rica?" I say, gently rubbing his back with my left hand. Ignacio draws another deep breath. Amiga suddenly leaps onto the bed and sits on Ignacio's lap where she buries herself.

"After prom, a group of us drove out to the beach to party. We went in three cars. Gwendolyn and I followed everyone in my little Jeep. We were young and silly and free. We had a bonfire at the beach and drank beer and chased one another. We played truth or dare. We shared stories. It was a great night," Ignacio says, his voice dipping.

"Just before 11 p.m., Gwendolyn called her parents to let them know that we were okay. Her dad urged her to be careful on the roads which were wet from an earlier heavy rainstorm. She told him that I was driving that night and she handed me the phone to reassure him. I told him, 'I'm a good driver. I know how slippery the roads can get. We will be careful, I promise.' "

"I believe you, Iggy. Your Jeep can easily flip over. Please be extra careful tonight, ok? '" her father told me.

"Wait a minute, who is Iggy?" I ask, interrupting the story.

A small smile forms on Ignacio's face.

"That's what my family and old friends call me. Can I continue with the story, Tommy?" Amiga suddenly barks at me.

"Sorry, please do, Iggy." I smirk.

"It was just after midnight. We were all leaving the beach to head back to the city. I followed the other two cars. And the last thing I remember, Gwendolyn and I were laughing, making our plans for the summer to go to New York. We were singing our favorite songs. And then I remember waking up in the hospital with bandages on my face and my right arm in a cast." Ignacio points to his arm which has two faint scars.

"My parents told me that morning that my car had struck something on the road and flipped over on a curve several times. Gwendolyn was thrown out of the Jeep and I slammed into my steering wheel. Her body was found a few feet away in the forest. She was declared dead at the scene, from what my parents told me."

"Oh my God, I am so sorry, Ignacio. I'm so sorry you had to go through that."

I lean my head on his shoulder.

"Thank you, Tommy. I still don't know how it happened. I still can't believe that Gwendolyn is gone. It's something that I have to live with for the rest of my life. My parents assured me it wasn't my fault. The roads in Costa Rica aren't the best especially after a rainfall. Gwendolyn's parents didn't blame me either but things became awkward with them, as expected. At the funeral, I sat in the back as Gwendolyn's loving family cried in the pews. I've been living with that guilt for more than 25 years. I killed my best friend," Ignacio says, wiping away a tear.

"But from what you're telling me, it was an accident. It wasn't your fault. Sometimes, things happen without rhyme or reason. I don't know why my mom got cancer but she did. Some things just are. I didn't know Gwendolyn but from what you've told me about her, I don't think she would want you living your life blaming yourself and carrying the weight of this guilt. That's no way to live. Is this why you take to the pills, Ignacio?"

He nods. His eyes continue to mist up.

"They help calm my anxiety which surfaces now and then. They also help me sleep. The pills help stuff down the pain. They keep it at bay. But the best medicine has been this little one. Amiga! She's my little shadow. No matter how bad or sad I feel, she lifts me up. Right, Amiga?" Ignacio says in his baby talk to the dog.

She playfully barks in agreement.

"For the record, I think Amiga lifts up anyone she encounters," I say with a smile, petting the top of the dog's head.

"Have you kept in touch with Gwendolyn's family?"

"My parents do. I don't visit Costa Rica as much as I used to. Too many memories, Tommy. I go for the holidays to see my siblings and nieces and nephews and that's about it."

"I can understand that. Maybe something that helped my friend Carlos in dealing with the loss of his mom can help you. He was always dreaming about her and an old friend of mine, a radio psychologist named Bella Solis suggested he should do something in her honor to celebrate her spirit. It's a way of taking that pain and converting it into something positive."

Ignacio's eyes light up with curiosity.

"What do you mean? What did your friend do to honor his mom?"

"Carlos created a beautiful spring garden at the high school where he teaches. His mother loved flowers and gardening in Miami so he decided to plant a garden with help from his students. At the end of his first year at the school, they had a special unveiling. I know because I was there and had to get *The Boston Daily* to cover it. Anyway, I can honestly say that the garden, its maintenance and its growth has helped Carlos heal in a way. I don't think he will ever get over the loss of his mother. But at least for Carlos, it's like a piece of his mother's spirit is there, with him at the school. And the garden is absolutely beautiful with radiant lilies, pansies and hydrangeas."

Ignacio leans closer to me and kisses me on the cheek.

"That sounds like a wonderful idea. Gwendolyn wasn't a big flower person except for the corsage she gave me at prom but maybe you're on to something. She loved living life and having great experiences."

"Maybe you can jump out of a plane to honor her? Make it an annual thing, on her birthday, to celebrate the life she lived and your friendship. I bet you she would like that." I grin.

Ignacio laughs, almost lost in thought of the memory of his plane jump with Gwendolyn.

"She knew how scared I was of jumping out of the plane. If anything, she would get a good laugh at seeing me doing it again, from wherever she is."

The idea brightens up Ignacio's eyes. He flashes his sexy smile. It warms my heart.

"Tommy, how did you honor your mom after she died? When you talk about Carlos, it almost sounds like you're talking about your experience as well."

I grin as I get up from the bed. I pluck a book from my shelf in the living room.

I then plop myself next to Ignacio and hand him the book, *Chicken Soup for the Cuban Soul.*

"What's this?" Ignacio leafs through the book which features dozens of feel-good short stories written by various authors. I point to the purple book marker.

"The Cuban Kitchen Dance by Tommy Perez, Dedicated to Gladys Perez," Ignacio reads the title of the chapter out loud.

"I wrote a short story about the time my mom taught me how to dance salsa, merengue and just about anything in our kitchen. My mother wasn't big on gardening like Carlos's but she loved to cha-cha-cha and dance," I say, motioning with my hands, moving my shoulders.

"Someone had forwarded me an email about the publisher looking for some Latino stories about growing up in a Latino home. The idea for the story just came to me. I was surprised when I received an email that it was going to be published. Besides my news articles, I never had something published in a book."

"This is so sweet, Tommy. What a beautiful gesture. Can I read it sometime?"

"Of course! You can borrow the book. It will give you something to read while I'm at Carlos's wedding. Maybe it will make you miss me, just a little bit," I say, holding my index finger to my thumb.

Ignacio twists his nose and smiles.

"Maybe just a little," he says, mimicking my gesture.

"Thank you for telling me about your friend, Ignacio. I hope you know you can tell me anything. I'm here to listen," I say, squeezing his upper shoulder with my hand.

"No, thank you Tommy. I'm glad I was able to share this with you."

We lean into one another and exchange a sweet warm kiss.

13

AHHH, MIAMI. AHHH, how I hate Miami. The tropical vapor wraps around me like a lasso that won't…let…go. As soon as I surface from the bustling terminal at Miami International Airport, I wipe away a sheen of sweat from my forehead and the back of my neck. I don't miss this smothering heat at all.

How did I survive summer all those years growing up here? How did I not dissolve into a puddle of sweat with only thick eyebrows and curly brown hair floating on the surface? It hasn't been 10 minutes that I've been here and the back of my cotton short-sleeved blue shirt has stuck to my back like another layer skin. The insides of my right palm that clench my backpack glisten with sweat. As I hold up the zipped bag that contains my suit, I glance at it and think how it must be cooler in there than out here. And to think Carlos's wedding is outside this weekend.

Why did he pick South Florida during the summer to get married? Boston would have been a lot cooler and closer. Correction, even Washington DC would have been more tolerable compared to here. These thoughts swim (because they are drenched in sweat too) through my head as I wait for my Uber ride.

According to the app, my designated chauffeur is named Cheryl. Within five minutes, a black Toyota Camry hybrid pulls up and a friendly middle-aged woman with straight blonde hair lowers the passenger side window.

"Hi there! Are you Tommy?" she says, chewing gum.

"That's me!" I wave.

"Well, hop on in!" she gestures with a slight drawl.

I prop open the rear passenger door and climb in with my suit bag and backpack. I check my right front pocket to make sure that the small box containing Carlos and Nick's wedding bands are still there.

"Have you been waiting long outside because you're drenched like a puppy that fell into a pool?"

"Sorry about that. I just got here from Boston. I'm readjusting to the Miami heat," I say, relieved to feel the air conditioner.

"No worries, Tommy. I'll crank up the AC as high as it goes for you. Here's some water to cool you down." She passes me a small bottle of water.

I hold it up and smile.

"Thanks Cheryl!"

"And one more thing, welcome to Miami! Now sit back and enjoy the ride and I'll get you to where you need to go." She then pulls the Camry out of the terminal and merges with the rest of the airport traffic toward LeJeune Road. We're off to my father's condo in downtown Miami.

Twenty minutes later, Cheryl drops me off at the 15-story waterfront high rise, one of many that seem to have sprouted overnight in the city's Brickell financial district. I wave to the security guard who recognizes me and he buzzes me in without me having to use the spare FOB.

My sneakers screech against the gleaming marble-tiled lobby as I enter the mirrored-elevator. I press '10' for my dad's floor. During the brief ride, I think of how my mom would have hated living here if she were alive. She adored our childhood home in mid-Miami Beach. It was her three-bedroom house, painted in a butter-yellow hue with white trimmings. A big gardenia bush stood in the front yard. My cousins, aunts and uncles regularly dropped by unexpectedly because my mom made them feel at home there. Whomever came over, she always had a flan ready to serve from the refrigerator. Often, my family and I would catch my mom dancing by herself with an invisible partner in the kitchen which was the inspiration for my short story. To me, my mom was the definition of home, a cocoon of love and support. Not this place, an overpriced tower filled with posers and wanna-be yuppies driving the latest sports and luxury car that they probably can't afford anyway except for Memorial Day or Labor Day car lease specials. This is one of the reasons I don't visit Miami often. I clash with the new Miami of gleaming and glittering skyscrapers, surgically enhanced women and men and their be-there, be-seen, gotta-go lifestyle that folks here seem to subscribe to. I don't like the chorus of constant cars honking and the ballet of construction cranes that dot the skyline like a mini New York. I don't like the exclusivity of Miami, the A-list this, the B-list that. To me, Miami was always a gay romantic desert. There was a new hot tourist around the corner to compete with.

I also don't like coming here out of principle. My father and sister went against my wishes to sell our house after my mom died. The house was paid off. There was no need to sell it. But my sister, who has always been closer to my dad than I while I was on Team Mom, talked him into selling the house and starting anew in downtown where real estate has boomed in recent years. Even though this place was bought with my dad's money from the sale of the house, it's really my sister's condo. It's her way of living that highlife she always fantasized about and that so many other Miamians want nowadays. Maine is my home now and will be for a long time if I can help it.

The elevator comes to a quick gentle stop. The doors swiftly open. I step out and walk on the hallway's plush green carpeting. I fidget with my keys and open the condo's front door and catch the view of Biscayne Bay through the sliding glass doors. The sun light slices through the place, warming the entire condo. I immediately call out to my dad and sister but no one seems to be home. All I hear is the mechanical hum of the central air conditioner. I spot a note on the dining room table.

It reads, *Welcome back Tommy! We'll be home soon. We're running some errands. We'll bring you dinner. Love, your big sis and dad!* "

Whatever. I crumple up the paper and toss it into the kitchen trash. I then head to my dad's bedroom and drop off my things and hang up the bag with my suit.

I sniff the inside of my sweaty T-shirt and realize that I definitely need to shower before I head over to la doctora Bella's book reading in Coral Gables or I may scare away her customers with my stank.

It's 7:15 p.m. and the aroma of fresh coffee and baked goods greet me as I walk inside Books and Books. I enter one of the salons and catch the tail end of Bella's event. The crowd of mostly Latinas applauds as Bella thanks everyone for attending.

"I'm so grateful that so many of you took time out of your busy Thursday to come to my reading, especially with this muggy weather, " she says gracefully from the podium.

She then spots me standing in the back and winks.

"And I want to thank my dear old friend Tommy Perez who has written beautiful articles about me and my work. He's hiding in the back. Everyone, say Hi to Tommy!" she declares. Women in their 50s and 60s to younger 20-year-old somethings suddenly turn around, look my way and smile. Some say hi. How embarrassing. I sheepishly grin back and wave to everyone. My cheeks warm.

"I will be around for a few minutes to sign some books so please, feel free to come up and say Hi. Thank you everyone," she says.

The crowd scatters and begins to form a line at a table stacked with her books. I linger in the back and patiently hang out as everyone gathers around la doctora who hugs each person who approaches her. While I wait, I check my smartphone. There's a message from Danny.

BEST MAN! I'm in Key West but where are thou Tomas Perez?

My lips curl up. I thumb back a response.

Tomas Perez is alive and well in Miami. He'll be down there first thing in the morning. In the meantime, take some photos of the beautiful sunset down there. You can't miss it. And check out Mallory Square. There's always a scene there. You'll have plenty to shoot besides Carlos and Nick.

Danny replies, *Aye aye captain! See you tomorrow. Drive carefully, BEST MAN!*

I will. And one more thing, don't call me Tomas Perez. ☺ I type back.

To which Danny replies, *Got it. BEST MAN!*

I begin checking my Facebook and Instagram accounts when I notice a text message from Ignacio.

Hey guapo! I just read your short story. So sweet. Does this mean you can dance? You'll have to show me sometime. Amiga and I already miss you. ☺

I awe to myself and place my right hand on my heart.

I'll be back before you know it. I'll send you some pix from the ceremony. Say Hi to Amiga for me! I text back.

And then an image pops up in my message box. It's a picture of Amiga sporting red sunglasses. I grin at the photo.

"What's so funny, Tommy?" Bella says warmly approaching me, suddenly interrupting my thoughts. "Come here and give your doctora a big hug!"

"Oh! Hi Bella! So good to see you." I hug her back, sliding the phone away into my back pocket.

"You look great, Tommy. Maine seems to agree with you. You're glowing or is that from the heat? Have you met someone special?" she says with a knowing grin.

"Damn, you're good! I have, sort of. I could never hide anything from you. Maybe you were a reporter in another life."

"Perhaps because I ask a lot of questions and I have some for you, my friend. I know how to read people and you're radiating good energy. Well, here I am. I'm all yours. Would you like to go to the café and catch up?" I smile and nod.

She laces her arm in the crook of my elbow like a mother or grand-mother would and escorts me to a corner table for two in the café area of the store.

I pull out a seat for Bella.

"What a gentleman, Tommy Perez!" Bella says, tucking some of the strands of her hair behind her ears. I grin as I take my seat.

A waitress appears and hands us menus.

"Just a latte for me, dear," Bella says, smiling at the waitress.

I order a double espresso. The waitress scribbles our orders on her notepad and disappears into the coffee bar area.

Bella leans in, her eyes brimming with warmth and love. She pats my right hand with hers which makes her bracelets jiggle.

"So tell me, what is going on in your life besides work? Your doctora is here so talk, young man!" she says, tapping her hand against the table.

I playfully roll my eyes and smirk.

"Well..."

Bella pivots her head and studies me.

"I know there's a guy in your life, maybe two, right?"

I twist my nose. Huh?

"Since you can read me so well, then you know everything. I don't have to say anything," I chide her, looking away.

"I'm intuitive Tommy, not psychic. Who is making you smile so much?"

I begin to tell her about Ignacio and our dates, Amiga.

"That sounds wonderful, Tommy. I'm glad you met someone. I was beginning to worry that you were never going to move on from Mikey. I know how much he meant to you in Boston."

The moment she says Mikey, I immediately think of his ocean-blue eyes, his light brown straight hair, the way he would bite down on his tongue whenever he laughed or wanted to make a point.

"But this guy, Ignacio, right? He sounds more mature and stable. I sense you might have a good thing here, Tommy. Take things slowly. Let the relationship or whatever you guys are doing unfold naturally."

The waitress returns with our drinks. I grab my cup of espresso and blow the steam from the top.

"Thank you, Bella. Yes, things are going well but I found these anti-depressants in his bathroom the other day. Ignacio then told me he's been taking them because his best friend died in a car accident when he was in high school. I appreciate the fact that he told about his friend and the pills but something is bothering me about it and I don't know what."

"First of all, he told you and that's a big step. He gets points for that in my book. There is a lot of stigma around people taking antide-pressants. I know that could not have been easy for him. I think that you're worried that you may have another Mikey situation. Mikey had issues with alcohol, right? And Ignacio takes these pills and that con-cerns you, no?"

Why do I suddenly feel like I'm the one being interviewed for once?

"I don't think he's addicted to them. Ignacio takes them everyday. They help him deal with his anxiety."

"Pay attention to that little voice inside you, Tommy. That's your spirit saying to be careful, be aware," she says, taking a sip of her latte.

"You're a good guy, my friend. You're doing great. Keep your eyes open and listen to your heart and that little voice. You've come a long way. I am so proud of you."

She cups my hands in hers and squeezes. Again, I feel her flow of positive energy.

I glance down at my espresso and grin. If Bella had a super power, it would be that she can see through anyone and pick up on anything. She has X-ray vision for the soul.

"So you're here for Carlos's wedding? Please send him my regards. He too has come a long way. I am glad to hear that both of you are still there for each other in Boston, I mean Maine or Boston. You know what I mean."

"He's my best friend and I'm his best man. I'm meeting up with Danny to show him around Key West tomorrow."

"Danny?" Bella asks, sipping her drink.

"I'm sorry. Danny is Carlos's photographer for the wedding. He's a really good guy. We've happened to work on some assignments together for the magazine."

Small pangs of joy rush over me as I go on to tell her about Danny, how he calls me BEST MAN in his brusque way and how much fun we've had on our stories in recent weeks, how I met him at Rico's wedding.

"Ay no!" Bella blurts out, clapping her hand.

"What Bella? What did I say?"

She shakes her head and clicks her tongue.

"What, what?" I say, almost sounding like an owl.

"That's guy number 2. You like this guy, too."

"He's been a cool friend. We have so much in common with the journalism. He can be annoying and fun at the same time, if that makes sense."

"No wonder you're glowing. You like two guys at the same time!"

"Nooooo...Danny is more in the friend zone."

"And what does he look like, Tommy?"

I stare off over Isabel's shoulder and describe Danny's blue eyes, dark hair, dimples and broad friendly smile. I sigh.

"See…you're attracted to him! I think it's wonderful that you have found another new friend who has similar professional interests. But please be careful with him and Ignacio. You seem fond of both of them, maybe a little more with Danny just based on your dreamy facial expressions when you talk about him and the way your voice just went up. And you're going to be spending time with him in the most romantic of occasions – a wedding! Don't get me wrong. I believe you like Ignacio and he sounds like a good guy. You need to figure out what who you want as a friend and as a potential boyfriend. No one likes to be in a love triangle. It's not fair to anyone including you."

She leans in and says in a low voice.

"Just be honest with both of them and yourself, Tommy. Listen to that beautiful spirit of yours."

Bella rubs the top of my right hand and smiles.

"And remember, Tommy," she continues.

"I know, I know. I have the power to change," I say all smart-alecky.

Bella beams.

"And I also have the power to bottom," I joke. I cover my mouth and stifle a laugh.

To that, Bella lifts her right eyebrow and shoots me a sidelong stare.

"Now, that's a whole over conversation for another time, Tommy."

14

THE WHIR OF chain saws (or are those scooters?) thunders over Duval Street, the main drag in the heart of Key West although I wouldn't be surprised to learn that there was a drag queen named Duval somewhere around here too. That's what Key West has always been known for, a place to escape to, the southernmost point of the United States where you can be anyone you want to be and no one bats an eyelash. That may explain why so many fugitives descend on Key West as a way to elude the authorities but that's another story perhaps a story for the local paper.

But I still think there's something magical about the Keys. Maybe it's having the Atlantic Ocean on one side and the Gulf of Mexico on the other. The ocean's colors unfold like a liquid quilt with changing blues. The water is bluer, more azure than in Maine or Miami. The air crisper, flowing with heat.

There's also something about the warm breeze brushing up against your face or blowing through your hair as if this were all part of a Mother Nature cleanse.

So here I am, joining sun-burned tourists, some shirtless, others in flip flops, who stream by me like a human river as I drive toward the hotel. I'm meeting up with Danny and the rest of Carlos's family and guests.

As I pass rows of T-shirt shops, boutiques and bars housed in former two-story wooden homes, I think about how I haven't seen Danny lately but he's been on my mind especially after what Bella said at the coffee shop yesterday. Although I'm attracted to him and at times his brusque personality, I've slotted him into the friend category. I already have eyes and perhaps some feelings for Ignacio. I wouldn't want to do anything to screw that up even though the relationship (ok, the situation or whatever we are) is budding.

Images of Ignacio and then Amiga flash in my mind as I continue driving when I suddenly have to slam on my brakes to avoid hitting a rooster. Yes, a rooster! The bird doesn't even flinch from my screeching tires. The rooster then continues casually crossing the road without a care in the world. Gripping the steering wheel, I shake my head and wait for the livestock to reach the other side of Duval. Wait, did it just glare at me? I shake my head side to side and keep on driving.

When I finally pull up to the hotel, there's a certain someone snapping photos as I parallel park. I nod up and wave to him.

"Perfect BEST MAN! Now, can you do that again but look at me from the side?" he shouts with gusto from the sidewalk.

To that, I flash my middle finger.

"Now snap this!" I smirk. I can't help it but I start to laugh as I grab my bag and suit from the back of my Ford rental sedan. Danny somehow entertains me with his teasing ways. I do like the attention although I can do without the BEST MAN tag line.

"Welcome to *Cayo Hueso* as you native Floridians like to call it. See, I've already learned some new words, BEST MAN!"

"And do you know what the Spanish word is for super annoying, Danny?"

Danny pauses for a second, scratches his chin and looks up at the bright blue cloudless sky.

"Um, no but I'm sure you'll teach me by the end of the trip. Need some help with your bags? Actually, on second thought, you seem like you've got that covered."

I heave a sigh and roll my eyes.

Danny continues photographing me (I don't know why) as I walk toward him and the hotel's main entrance with my luggage in tow. I must look a mess. It's hotter down here than in Miami and I'm already wiping my face with the sleeve of my shirt. I can feel my hair mushrooming into a hedge.

"You missed a spot. Just kidding, Tommy! It's good to see you here. By the way, the groom-to-be is with his family and he said for me to meet up with you while he hangs out with them. So I guess it's just you and me for a bit," Danny says, patting my sweaty back. His blue eyes twinkle with excitement.

I smile as we walk into the hotel toward the front desk.

"How will I survive being all alone with you, Mr. Irresistible, NOT!" I say, my voice laced with sarcasm as I place my free hand over my heart.

I then remotely lock the doors of the car. When I look back toward the sidewalk, I notice the rooster from earlier strutting like a feathered diva. It looks my way. Did it just glare at me again? Welcome to Key West.

After dropping off my suit and bag in my room, which is painted in soothing soft whites and blue, I change into a sleeveless red shirt and a pair of shorts. I lock my door and head to the lobby to meet up with Danny.

"So what's the plan, Tommy?" he says, standing in his Bermuda green shorts and white tank top which outlines his lean frame.

His face and shoulders are pinkish, sunburned.

"I know it's hot but I thought we could just, you know, walk around or rent some bikes. That's the best way to see the city, which is about the size of South Beach."

"I'm game! Whatever you want to do is cool with me."

He pats me on the shoulder.

We ask the front desk clerk about bike rentals and the middle-aged freckled man happily tells us that the hotel has some bikes for guests. To that, Danny offers a thumbs up. I pretend to take a picture of him with an invisible camera.

"You need to bring them back by 5 p.m. or you'll be charged the day rate, which is $25," the clerk informs us.

I salute him in a smart alecky way as he hands us the keys to the bikes' locks. I pick the red bicycle and Danny chooses the blue one. As we carefully wheel them out of the lobby and onto the sidewalk, our bicycling adventure begins.

Side by side, we pedal along Duval Street, passing the same boutiques, bars, and tourist shops that I saw earlier. Fellow tourists on scooters zip around us. The sun pounds off the asphalt, creating a hazy vapor.

An idea pops inside my head and I turn to Danny.

"I know where we can go. Follow me!"

Danny mimics the salute that I had done earlier with the front desk clerk. We make a right on Olivia Street and head toward Passover Lane where a black ironed fence encircles the property.

We navigate through a small paved road lined with tall flowing palm trees. They are the only living things here besides us cyclists.

"Um, Tommy, I think we made a wrong turn. This looks like a cemetery," Danny says, swallowing hard. We make our way deeper into the city's cemetery which is filled with crumbling above-ground tombstones.

"You win the daily double, Danny! Yep, this is a cemetery but it feels more like an old urban park that just happens to have a lot of tombstones. Just look at the palms!"

"And why are we here, Tommy? Is this where you bury the bodies of your former dates?"

I narrow my eyes at him.

"Nooo… just annoying photographers. Actually, I do know a guy that is buried here. Just kidding. Anyway, I thought you'd appreciate this because there are so many stories here." I pull my bike over to look at a boxy white tombstone.

"See, Danny! The dead have stories to tell here," I say, pointing to the rows of other crypts.

"And the same goes for the living. How did you hear about this place? It's not in the center of town or anything."

I explain that during previous trips, I always rode my bike by the cemetery and enjoyed reading the various inscriptions, some of which are quirky and funny. I know it's bad form to make fun of the dead but what if they're the ones poking fun at themselves?

I think that's why people come here, to see the mix of history and humor.

"You really know how to treat a guy, BEST MAN!"

"Why, thank you. Just something different to see and photograph. Another side of Margaritaville. Not everything here is about partying."

We make our way deeper into the cemetery and ride slowly enough to read the various epitaphs.

There's one which serves as a memorial to the crew former battleship the USS Maine that sank off Havana Harbor in 1898. Another pays tribute to the Cuban Martyrs for their failed revolution against Spain in 1868. But then there are the humorous epitaphs. One reads *He Loved Bacon* while another declares *I Told You I Was Sick.*

"Oh dear, there's even one for a pet deer. You've got to see this," Danny calls out, gesturing for me to come his way.

He photographs this particular grave which is dedicated to a deer named Elfina. A four-legged figurine sits at the top of the tombstone.

"Well, she had a good life. She was born in Coral Gables and she lived to be 14!" I shrug and hold my hands up. Being the goof that I am, I then lay down next to the animal statue and Danny gladly takes a photo. I ask him to email me a copy. I want to send it to Ignacio when I have a chance later.

"Rest In Peace, Elfina!" Danny says, with a hand over his heart. I repeat the same gesture as we stand over the grave.

As we continue reading and riding, the smell of coconut tanning oil permeates the air. The place is eerily quiet and creepy yet radiates a Zenful like calm. When we reach the end of the road in the cemetery, I notice a chicken strutting in front of me. I smile to myself.

"What's so funny, Tommy? Did I miss another tombstone for a deer?" Danny turns to me.

"Nah, it just hit me that the only things that are alive and well in old Key West are these roaming roosters," I say, flapping my arms like chicken wings.

As if on cue, the livestock leaps onto my front tire and stares at me with its black and yellow eyes. I quickly lean back because I don't know what it's going to do. Danny then quickly captures the awkward spontaneous moment with his camera.

"I have to post this on Instagram and share it with Carlos. I'll add *Looking for Cock with the one and only Tommy P!* as the caption or how about *How fowl!*"

I cringe inwardly at Danny's bad pun.

"What am I going to do with you?" I say, holding up my hands in frustration. To which, he snaps a photo, of course.

I think I could get used to this, being friends with Danny. He's fun to hang around. And despite my physical attraction for him, I really like him as a friend. There's no pressure or awkward moments. We actually gel pretty well as pals. I don't think I would be jealous if he were to date another guy. In fact, I'd be happy to see him with a guy who made him as happy as his ex-boyfriend once did.

As these thoughts fill my mind, we make a U-turn at the end of the cemetery and head back toward the entrance.

"Now that we've survived the dead, let's race over to the beach where the ceremony will be held tomorrow. Then we'll rest up at the hotel and call it a day because I...am...beat! Tomorrow is Carlos's big day."

"And yours too. You're the...wait for it...BEST MAN!"

With that, I speed away, turn around and stick out my tongue at Danny.

"Hey, wait up. I don't know how to get back!" he shouts back.

It's just before 4 p.m. on the BIG day and I'm in Carlos's hotel suite helping him with last minute touches. As soft tropical instrumental Cuban music plays in the background, I tighten his pink bow tie and straighten out the back of his navy blue suit. I wrap some scotch tape around my hand to pick up any stray lint from his jacket.

"You look handsome, my friend. As always!" I say, tilting my head and grinning. I swell with pride. It feels good to see someone I know feeling so happy, being connected and loved by someone who feels the same way about him. Maybe one day I will find that special connection as well.

"Thanks, loco. I can't believe this is happening and to top it off, my family is here. I like to think that my mom is also here in spirit, watching over me. I can feel her here, if that makes sense, Tommy."

"I think both our moms are here in their own way, watching us. They're probably sitting around here somewhere drinking cafecito and gabbing about us to each other. " Tears begin to well in my eyes. I try to will them back.

"Oh no, loco! Don't get all mushy on me now. You're going to make me cry before the ceremony even starts and I'm going to have boogers coming out of my nose as I walk down the aisle and that's not what I want on my wedding day. No way!"

"I'm not being mushy. I think I have something in my eyes," I say to Carlos, rubbing my eyes with my knuckles as if something were irritating them. I open one eye and smirk at my friend. I'm a horrible actor.

We laugh.

I turn Carlos around in front of the mirror and stand behind him. I place my hands over his shoulders and squeeze. I then rest my head over his right shoulder.

"You...look...perfect! I think it's time, Carlos. Your husband-to-be awaits."

"Let's do this, loco!" he says, with a clap.

As we begin to walk out of the suite to head toward the beach, Danny appears in the hallway and snaps some photos of Carlos.

"Muy muy guapo, Carlos!" Danny shouts out, rolling the *r* in Carlos's name, which makes us laugh. Danny is sort of dressed for the occasion too, wearing blue jeans, a white T-shirt and grey sports jacket. Then again, he's the photographer working a job but he also feels like a guest too.

"You clean up well," I say.

"It was Elfina the deer. She gave me some suggestions yesterday at the cemetery." Exasperated, I just laugh it off.

As Carlos walks outside on this breezy sunny day across the street to the beach, his sister Mary joins us holding a bouquet of gardenias, her mother's favorite. Since their mom can't escort Carlos down the sandy aisle, Mary will fulfill that role even though they've never been the closest of siblings, another commonality that Carlos and I share.

"Are you ready, little brother?" she says, dressed in a lovely white dress that matches the bouquet.

He grins, seemingly speechless.

Rows of beige chairs are lined up along each side of the aisle filled with Carlos and Nick's families. The rows are marked with beautiful white gardenias which shake with the sea breeze.

At the makeshift altar that faces the Atlantic, I see Nick standing with his best man Gabriel. I wave to both of them. The strum of a guitar signals the beginning of the wedding march. The guests, a mix of Cuban Americans and Portuguese relatives dressed up in a sea of beige, grey and navy blue suits and dresses, stand up.

I wait my cue. Nick's parents and then Carlos's father walk down the path. As I begin my solo walk, I hold my head high as a slight smile forms on my lips. All the guests are looking at me and grinning back. Danny seemingly flies all over the ceremony like a human drone, capturing every photographic angle he could think of. As expected, he's doing a good job and I'm looking forward to seeing the pictures.

I stand on Carlos's side of the makeshift altar and wink at Nick and Gabriel.

I then look back at the beginning of the aisle where Carlos and Mary await their turn. It's time. A flurry of butterflies soars inside me and I'm not even the one getting married. Emotion tightens in my chest. I'm just excited for my loco friend.

I nod up and flash a thumbs up to Carlos. We trade smiles as he begins his march with Mary down the aisle. Once at the altar, she hugs him and gives him a kiss on the cheek.

"Good luck little brother. Nick is a good guy," I hear her say. She then settles into a seat in the front row next to Carlos's dad and his girlfriend.

A little teary eyed, my friend takes his place next to Nick before the reverend who begins the ceremony by welcoming the guests. As he speaks in English, some Spanish and bits of some Portuguese (to honor Nick's family), Carlos and Nick lovingly gaze into each other's eyes and hold hands. I finger my necktie, my fifth one, and smile.

15

"AND NOW, A few words from Carlos's best man, Tommy Perez!"
Mary introduces me inside the hotel reception hall. I walk up to the
long table where Carlos and Nick are seated and holding hands. The
table is topped with vases filled with beautiful gardenias. And in
front of the table is a monitor featuring a slide show of Carlos and
Nick's romance – day trips to Providence, the Pride festival in Boston,
canoe rides in New Hampshire, selfies in Miami. Mary and I hug as she
hands me the microphone. I look out at the dozen or so tables filled
with Nick and Carlos's families and friends.

Carlos and I trade winks. From my back pocket, I remove the
speech that I wrote or what Danny might call in his obnoxious way
THE BEST MAN SPEECH. Speaking of, flashes from Danny's camera
cause me to momentarily squint and I wave away the flashes like
pesky mosquitoes. The room falls to a quiet hush. All eyes are on me.
I focus, smile, inhale deeply and begin.

"What can I say about Carlos that you all don't already know? He
is the kindest person I have ever met, always willing to help someone
whether it's a student or a fellow teacher. When I first met Carlos, he
was a newcomer to Boston just as I was a few years before. He was shy
and sweet and a little lost because of a deep loss in the Martin family.
But as our friendship grew, I saw Carlos grow into the confident man

that he is today. He has made Boston his home and in doing that, he has found another home, one with a special guy, Nick Lanza." I smile at Nick.

"And it all began with one of our typical Friday nights at El Oriental de Cuba restaurant. Nick was there with his buddy Gabriel and I was there with mine. I'd like to think that Cupid conspired with Gabriel and me to get our best friends at the restaurant that night because he knew these two would make a great match if only their paths crossed. And it worked. Maybe it was Mr. Cupid. Maybe there was a special ingredient in their chicken and rice or mamey shake that night. Whatever it was, Carlos and Nick came to be that night. They soon learned that they were better together than apart. I'm so glad you guys found each other. I wish you all the best and a life-time of love and happiness. Let's toast to my favorite loco and his husband."

I raise my glass of champagne.

To that, everyone stands up and clinks their glasses which is fol-lowed by a chorus of applause. Carlos rises from his seat, followed by Nick and they walk toward me with outstretched arms.

"I love you, loco! How can I ever repay you?" Carlos says into my ear.

"Well, when I get married, you and Rico could embarrass the hell out of me with a double toast as my best men!" I pat his back.

"Deal, loco!" Carlos says, smiling and stepping to the side as Nick moves in for a hug too.

"That was great, Tommy. Thank you," Nick says, squeezing both my shoulders.

"I know my friend is in good hands with you. Take care of him."

"Of course. I love him with all my heart," Nick says, his hazel eyes twinkling with pride.

After we hug, I return to my seat, Danny flashes me a thumbs up and silently mouths BEST MAN! I make a silly face and settle back into my chair.

As the afternoon spills into night, the guests dance and mingle on a small rectangular dance floor to a mix of music from Gloria Estefan and Shakira (some of Carlos's favorites) to pop and clubby hip hop from Jason DeRulo and Usher (Nick's choices.) I loosen up my necktie and dance with Carlos, his sister and their cousins as well as Gabriel and Nick. We all form a big circle. Everyone grooves in place as people clap and take turns showing off their moves in the middle of the group. It's all festive and fun with people hollering and laughing.

After an hour of busting my booty and attempting to look cool and suave on the dance floor, I stride to the open bar for a drink. I need to recharge my dancing batteries.

"I'll have whatever this dancing machine is having," a man's voice tells the college-age bartender.

I turn to my right and grin.

"Um, are you sure, Danny? I'm having a Vodka with Diet Coke. That doesn't sound like your type of drink."

"And are we watching our figure, BEST MAN? The wedding is over. Drink a beer. Have some carbs. Gain some weight. Be wild and free. Your duties are officially OVAH for the night," Danny says, his eyes brightening.

I turn to the bartender.

"I'm still having the vodka with diet coke."

"Me too," Danny interjects. "I should take my own advice and be wild and free. I rarely drink but this is a special occasion."

The bartender serves us our twin drinks. We each take sips and gaze out at the dance floor.

"Look at those two," Danny nods toward Carlos and Nick who begin to slow dance to Ed Sheeran. "The love just pours out of their eyes."

"I know. I think they were meant to be together. True love. It's so rare but it can happen," I say wistfully. I twirl my straw in my drink as I watch my friend and his husband exchange loving glances. They're swaying together and they look as one with their matching suits and ties.

"If the eyes are the windows to the soul, then Nick and Gabriel's say they are soul mates," I turn to Danny.

"Then yours a little fogged up because you're getting misty-eyed, Tommy."

"Oops sorry," I rub my eyes. "I'm just happy, not sad or anything. Weddings have that effect on me."

"It's cute, Tommy. You're cute," Danny says with a half smile.

The compliment catches me by surprise. Danny thinks I'm cute. But I'm not going to over analyze this or anything. We're friends and friends can call each other cute or sweet or whatever. It doesn't have to mean anything.

After the husbands finish their slow dance, the deejay announces on the microphone, "Let's hear it for Mr. and Mr. Martin-Lanza!" Everyone claps and cheers them on. Some guests whistle too.

"Now it's time to heat things up a bit, if you know what I mean. Come on everybody, it's time to feel HOT HOT HOT! You all know the song. You all know what to do," the deejay shouts on the microphone. I know the song. It's that 1980s party song by Buster Poindexter but I'm not sure I know what to do. Is there a special dance to this? Is this like the Macarena or Vogue?

The music starts to play and Danny and I look at each other with playful grins. We can't help but start laughing because suddenly, everyone marches or flocks to the dance floor as if an invisible Pied Piper commands them. They raise their hands and shout "HOT HOT HOT!" with animated faces.

Danny downs his drink and I do the same. He motions with his head for me to join him on the dance floor. I shrug my shoulders and say "Why not?"

And with that, we find a little space in the corner of the dance floor. We shake to the left, and then to the right. We lean forward and back. We jump three times when we hear "HOT HOT HOT!"

And then Danny does some sort of cha-cha-cha move that looks awkward and funny. I toss my head back, laugh and clap my hands.

"And...what...was...that, Danny?" I shout over the music as I groove in place.

"Oh just me feeling HOT HOT HOT," Danny shouts back, repeating the strange move which goes something like this: two steps to the right, two steps to the left, and some Twerking action while his hands remain in front of his chest.

"I think it's more like NOT NOT NOT!" I tease. Danny feigns dramatic offense as if I shot a hole in this heart. He then twists his nose at me.

Since we're having such a great time worthy of a selfie, I pull out my smartphone from my back pocket and pose with Danny. We wrap our arms around each other's shoulders, like old friends. We lean back with our super sized smiles as I angle my phone above us.

"Say HOT HOT HOT!" I gently bark. We both shout it and I snap the photo. I look it over and show it to Danny and he nods. I immediately share it on my Instagram account which is TOMMYPEREZWRITES. Of course, I add #HOTHOTHOT plus #carlosandnickwedding and #keywest.

We continue dancing, bumping our bums, snapping our fingers to the beat and just having fun.

Carlos and Nick eventually shimmy our way. The four of us hold hands and jump up and down like cheerleaders at a pep rally. (Hey, it is a gay wedding, after all!)

Laughter and giggles fill and charge the air around us. As I watch this joyous scene, I think to myself, this is exactly how I would want to celebrate my own wedding some day. I want to be surrounded by the love of my friends (in this scenario, Rico would be here too dancing away with Oliver) and family.

And I know the perfect photographer to capture the occasion, my awkward but funny dance partner, Danny or Mr. HOT HOT HOT, NOT NOT NOT!

16

I'M STILL RECOVERING from Carlos and Nick's wedding. My legs throb with soreness from the bike riding and of course, all the booty shaking with Danny. My calf muscles feel tight and tender like tennis balls. And what the hell did I do to my butt? My butt cheeks are sore too. Maybe from all the Twerking and my unsuccessful attempts at crunking or just looking cool. These thoughts hum through my head as I drive back to Ogunquit from Logan airport. The weather is perfect, a sunny, cool and breezy Friday afternoon as I'm about to hop off I-95 to Route 1 toward home.

As I cross the New Hampshire toll at the Massachusetts border, my phone pings that there's a new text message. With my right hand, I grab my smartphone and glance at the message. It's Ignacio.

Hola sexy! Are you back yet? the message reads.

I carefully thumb a reply.

Hey you! Almost. I should be home in about 20 minutes or so.

He types back, *Once you're settled in, stop by the inn. I want to see you. We missed you.* ☺

I'll text you when I'm on my way. TTYL

He responds with *XOXOXO*

As I pass the antique shops and seafood shacks in York, I wonder, what is Ignacio up to? I smell a surprise. Blame it on my journalistic instincts. It's like my Spidey sense and I can't turn it off. My mind immediately begins to conjure up potential plans. But I must admit, I'm looking forward to seeing Ignacio's handsome face and of course, Amiga. Being away from them made me realize that we're like a little family or the beginning of one.

After Carlos and Nick's wedding, I'm more inspired to have my own. If two of my best friends and others who I know have found love and happiness with that special guy or someone, then why can't I have my brass ring or wedding ring some day? Is my turn at the altar coming up? Did Cupid dispatch Ignacio my way in Maine? For that reason, could Ignacio be...the one? I gulp. And did some higher power send Danny my way to remind me of the potential romance with Mr. Costa Rica?

The questions tumble in my head like laundry in a dryer. I finally pull into the short driveway of my Cape Cod-style apartment building.

After luxuriating in a long hot shower - oh those feel so good especially after a three and half hour flight! – and unpacking my clothes, I dab some cologne and neatly comb my hair.

I look at myself in the mirror and I notice that my face is sun-burned, more like sun kissed from the trip. My nose and cheeks glow pink as if I'm blushing. I kind of like it. Mother Nature's make up. I do one last review (clean shaven, groomed hair, thick eyebrows some-what symmetrical and I quickly pluck some stray grays from my the front of my hairline) and I'm ready to meet up with Ignacio. I message him that I'm on my way. He responds with a smiling emoticon.

About 20 minutes later, I'm inside the inn strolling down the hallway toward Ignacio's room. Soft barks echo from the end of the hallway. Hmmm. I wonder who that could be? The woofs-woofs grow louder as I approach his door. Just as I'm about to knock, the white door slowly swings open. Amiga rushes toward me like a greyhound launching from the starting gate of a race. She leaps toward me and paws at my knees. Smiling, I bend down and softly rub her ears.

"See, she really missed you, Tommy. And so did I," Ignacio says warmly, widening the doorway to let me in. He moves in and softly settles his lips over mine which I gladly accept. I draw him into a hug and inhale his grassy lemony cologne. When he pulls away, he smiles which makes his eyes crinkle.

"Welcome back home!" Ignacio says, stepping back and pointing to the window where there's a banner that reads *Welcome back Tommy Perez!* A red and orange balloon bob in each corner of the window which is lighted by the glimmering afternoon sunlight. From the pocket of his blue cargo shorts, Ignacio suddenly grabs a handful of confetti and tosses it into the air. The tiny paper sprinkles down on all of us. Amiga jumps up and down trying to lick the confetti. I cover my mouth and giggle.

"Why thank you. This is so so sweet but I was only gone a few days. It's not like I came back from war or something." I lean in and kiss Ignacio again. The touch of our lips sends insatiable tingles that ripple throughout my body.

"Oh my God! You didn't have to do this, Ignacio!"

I take in the whole scene and move closer to the banner which is written in rainbow hues. I wave my hands to keep the confetti floating in the room. Then I grab one of the balloons and hold it.

"We wanted to! It was Amiga's idea. Once she sets her mind on doing something, I just follow along." Amiga playfully barks. Ignacio then scoops her up in his arms like a baby.

"She even made me the sign! She has good handwriting, no? She wanted you to know that you are always welcomed in our home even though we live in a hotel room. Our room is your room!" Ignacio grins, holding up Amiga's right paw.

"That sounds good to me!" I say, leaning over and petting Amiga's white furry head. She licks my palm.

"I'm beginning to feel at home here too. Thanks again."

My heart swells with pride at this scene. The little flame I carry for Ignacio continues to grow.

The only other homecoming that I've ever had was when my mom would greet me with her famous flan when I opened the front door of our house after arriving from Boston. It became my welcome back home to Miami tradition. My dad and sister would pick me up from the Miami airport and my mom waited at the house to surprise me with her caramel-dripping flan. It was a surprise the first time she did it.

After that trip, I pretended to be surprised because I could see the joy and love that radiated from her hazel eyes and her big smile whenever she opened the door with the dessert. She also shouted "SURPRISE!" when I opened the door. But with her thick Spanish accent, it sounded more like "SOOO...PRIZE!"

Oh, Mami, I miss you.

"Hey Tommy, are you okay? You look like you're deep in thought, a little sad. Did I say something wrong? Is this too much?" Ignacio says with concern. He gently places Amiga back down on the carpet.

I place my hand on his right shoulder.

"Oh no. You did everything right. This is wonderful, really. This big welcome just reminded me of something. Actually, more like some-one, my mom," I say wistfully. I explain her welcome home tradition.

Ignacio gives me a sweet embrace and kisses my neck. He rubs his hands along the planes of my back which comforts me.

I melt in his arms.

"I'm sorry, Tommy. The more you talk about your mom, the more wonderful she sounds. I'm glad this brought back a good memory."

Sensing my bittersweet feeling, Amiga trots over to me and sits on my feet. This dog! She is too much. She then looks up at me.

"You're such a good girl, Amiga, you know that?" I say in my dog-gie baby talk which I've picked up from Ignacio.

Once again, she barks in agreement. My mood lightens up again. It's good to be back in Ogunquit.

Following the surprise welcome from Ignacio and Amiga, the three of us stroll along Marginal Way toward Perkins Cove. When we arrive at the foot bridge, I marvel at all the fishing and commercial boats gliding to and from the cove and the open water. The salty scent of the ocean permeates the air around us. I deeply inhale it, imagining the air cleansing my lungs and spirit. This is one of my favorite spots in town because of the picturesque views and the soothing breezes.

From this perch, I like to gaze at the inns and homes and their verdant lawns across the channel. I often wonder, what it must be like to own such an estate.

"Tommy, hello! Maine to Tommy Perez! I think you're lost in thought again." Ignacio looks at me with a half smile.

Slightly embarrassed, I scratch my head and turn to him.

"Oops, sorry about that. I did it again. I was just admiring the houses over there and what it must be like to live in such a big space. Except for my parent's house, I've only lived in small apartments. That's New England for you! Scratch that. That's living on a journalist salary."

Ignacio gently rubs my back with his left hand. Amiga nuzzles her body in between our legs.

"One day, I will have a small cottage where I can grow my own avocados and vegetables in my backyard and where Amiga can run free. A hotel room isn't the best place for a little dog. But that's for now, temporary."

Oh.

My eyebrows furrow. My heart suddenly pounds.

"Temporary? Are you planning on moving or something, Ignacio?"

He looks down at Amiga with a smile and pets her head. His eyes then meet mine again.

"As much as I like it here during the summer, I don't want to be here for the winter. I have never been a fan of the cold weather. I'm from Costa Rica after all." He grins which makes his eyes crinkle again in that special way.

"This was more of a seasonal job, to help out my friend. I have to start thinking about what to do and where to go next. Maybe it's time to go back to Miami, Orlando or try some place new."

Amiga suddenly glances up at Ignacio when he says Miami.

Ignacio looks ahead at the dark blue water and the rocks that line the channel. I look at him and then down at Amiga and then the reality hits me like one of those waves that surfers ride along Ogunquit beach. Whatever we are and whatever we are doing, it's fleeting like a New England season. This may be just a summer fling. Maybe I shouldn't invest too much into the relationship since he's planning on moving away anyway. I never believed in long-distance relationships.

I never understood why a couple couldn't stay in the same city or at least in the same state if they really wanted to stay together.

Perhaps I just should take a step back emotionally and take things day by day with Ignacio because one day at the end of the summer, he may just declare: "Tommy, I'm moving to LA, Brazil, or wherever city. It was nice knowing you this summer!" I do my best to will away these thoughts so I can at least continue enjoying the view before me as well as the rest of the afternoon with Ignacio and Amiga. We may not have that many left.

As we stand there, I realize that this is what happens when you open up your heart. You also open it up to pain.

17

AHHH BOSTON! MY old home. I'm on assignment here to interview the costume designer for the new newspaper-drama inspired
by the real Boston reporting team for its award-winning coverage of
priests who were longtime rampant pedophiles. Although the action
in the movie takes place in 2002, the designer had to make the five
actors dress like they were in that time period which also looks very
1990s. Clothing styles leaned toward baggie pants and loose-fitting
shirts. But no matter the year, the unofficial dress code for Boston
journalists especially for men has always been Polo-type shirts and
khakis pants.

I should know. I used to wear those to work when I was reporter
at the paper (although I also liked navy and tan corduroy pants.)
Coincidentally, I'm wearing khakis pants and a light blue button down
shirt and brown loafers.

A press junket is being held in the auditorium of the newspaper,
my old stomping ground. As I park my Volkswagen in the grand parking lot studded with boxy green delivery trucks, I grab my notepad
with my list of questions, my digital recorder and my press creden-
tials. Before I walk inside, I sit in my car and gaze at the paper's
red-bricked building. Flashes of my earlier years as a reporter or PP
(pre-*People*) envelope me like a swirl of fall-time leaves.

I vividly remember my first day at work here. I wore a light blue Polo shirt and khakis pants (I wasn't joking about the unofficial dress code) and sauntered into the security office with a big old smile on my face for my press pass photo. My first article was a profile on a Harvard graduate student who took in foster babies and brought them to her classes. Imagine a screaming baby sitting in the arms of a sweet 22-year-old student who comforted the baby with one hand while taking notes with another. When the story printed that Sunday, I immediately ran to CVS in Harvard Square and bought several copies. I mailed each to my family and friends. I also framed the piece in my studio. That article led to hundreds of other stories about Boston, Cambridge and New England. I also recall sharing some of the stories with Mikey. But when I showed them to him, he had already read them.

"I read your stories online, Tommy. That way, I'm one of the first people to read your stuff. I'm your biggest fan. So is my family," he once told me when I had another story I wanted to show him over coffee at Barnes and Noble in Braintree, our regular rendezvous point.

Although we had some rough times with his drinking, Mikey could charm the pants off me, literally. Those unexpected compliments always put me in a happy haze. It was those little acts of kindness from Mikey that made me love and appreciate him more.

Ahhh, Mikey. Ahhh, Boston. In my mind and heart, the two are entwined which is why I don't come to the Hub that often. Too many memories, too many reminders. Maine remains a fresh canvas for me. New memories, new experiences. Peace of mind. Tranquillity.

Those Boston memories accompany me as I step out of my car and stride toward the glass-encased entrance of the newspaper.

I present my *People* magazine ID to the security guard who immediately recognizes me.

"Well, look who it is! Tommy Perez! Man, how have you been?" Terrence says with a friendly laugh. He greets me with a handshake and a hug.

At six-feet-two and burly, Terrence dwarfs me and envelopes me into his big muscular arms. I pat him on the back which I could barely reach. (I'm barely 5-feet-nine inches tall.)

"We miss you around here now that you're in the big leagues, Tommy!" he says, as I pull away from the embrace.

"Awe. I miss you guys, too. It's good to be back. I'm here for the - "

"the movie about the pedophile priests!" he interrupts me. "Who isn't? We have all sorts of media in the auditorium. It's a circus in here. Just go ahead in. You know where to go."

I wink at him.

"Now you come back here before you leave. I want to hear all about your job and your family, ya hear? "

I salute him like a captain.

"Yes sirree. It's good seeing you, Terrence. I'll see you later."

I wave and then amble down the brightly-lit corridor that is lined with white painted bricks. I follow the signs for the media junket to the auditorium. Once there, I check in with a friendly clerk at a table.

"Welcome Tommy Perez! Cheryl Fields will be ready for you in about 10 minutes in the small office around the corner from the auditorium. We have refreshments and cookies for you while you wait. You can have a seat over there."

She points to a row of red-colored chairs. I thank her and head that way.

The chatter of other reporters, some local, others national, mix in with the mechanical buzz of the air conditioners. Wesley Harris, one of my colleagues at our sister entertainment publication is here too. He'll be doing the one-on-one interviews with the reporters and the actors who play them. That left me with the costume designer for online and print. With a few minutes to kill, I review my questions on my Post It. I also make sure my recorder has enough minutes left for the interview. Then my smartphone pings that I have a new text message.

I fish my phone out of my front pocket. It's a message from Rico. We start texting.

Gurrl, what breaking entertainment stories are you working on today?

Hey Rico! I'm in Boston, actually. At my old newspaper for a story.

Tommy in Boston? No way. You know what that means, right?

That I have a story to write in Boston? I text back.

Ha! You have to stop by our place and say Hi. Maybe we can have a drink at Club Café like old times. Being a married man, I don't get out much these days. I need my wingman and that's you, amigo.

I respond with a smiling face emoticon.

Once I'm done with my interview and transcribing it, I'll drop by and say Hi to you and Oliver.

I'll be home after 6. See you later, TP! He texts back.

After putting my phone on vibrate, the friendly clerk waves to me and alerts me that the costume designer is ready for me. I store my phone in my bag and make my way toward the small office where the interview will take place.

When I walk in, I see a petite 40-something-year-old woman with dark short black hair sitting in a chair under the bright fluorescent lights. She smiles and waves at me.

"Hello. You must be, Mr. Tommy Perez. I'm Cheryl. So nice to meet you," she says with a slight New York accent as she rises from her chair.

I shake her hand and settle into a chair in front of her.

"Same here, Cheryl." I pull out my digital record and make sure that the red light is on for recording. I grab a notepad from my messenger bag. I'm ready to go.

Then she grins at me again.

"I know you wanted to focus on the clothing style of the journalists but can I just say that you are wearing it today? You could have easily been an extra in the movie with your look."

I flash a big smile and look down. I never know how to handle compliments.

"And what look is that, exactly?" I cross my right leg over my knee and lean in.

"Like the journalists in the movie and in real life, the dress code is something you don't really think about. You have other things that are more important to focus on, such as your stories. So you dress in this unofficial uniform, khakis and an oversized shirt. Simple, casual and comfortable clothes to get through the day of hustling and bustling."

"Well, I think you just answered my first question, Cheryl. And I'll take your comments about my dress code as a good thing."

I scribble some more notes.

As the interview continues, I ask her about the challenges in making people look ordinary, whether she made the clothes or borrowed them from the actors, and did she have resistance from the cast in making them look, well, unglamorous as reporters.

She answers each question gracefully and thoughtfully. It turns out she recreated some of the journalists' clothing after studying photos of them during the time they were working on the stories. She also tells me how some of the actors, who are fit and slim, resisted at first in wearing loose-fitting clothes that hid their figures.

"Actors are a particular bunch. You have to work with them to appease their concerns. Unless their character is overweight, they don't want to look fat on film," Cheryl says with a smirk.

"Oh, are you talking about anyone in particular?" My eyebrows shoot up.

"Let's leave that in general terms. It's not just this movie but other productions I have been part of."

Thirty minutes later, my notepad is filled with the chicken scratch known as my handwriting. And I'm done. I thank Cheryl for her time and we shake hands. She gives me her card which has her cell phone in case I have any follow up questions.

After the interview, I decide to stroll around the newspaper like I used to when I was on a break from writing. (I know Terrence wouldn't have an issue with that.) I use the back stairwell to go up to the main newsroom floor. As I walk down the shiny hallway, I notice many empty cubicles that were once filled with classified ad clerks. As I pass the carpeted Features section, I see a handful of writers among a sea of empty desks that sit under a blinking fluorescent bulb that is about to go out.

When I worked here, the newsroom hummed with life, from ringing phones to reporters talking over one another during their interviews. Even the floor of the newsroom vibrated from the working presses down the hall. Now, this feels more like a library, or an empty mall.

It's sad to see the slow death of newspapers as they wither and shrink with advertising declines and staff cuts. As print journalism transitions to online which never seems to end, less reporters are needed and these grand bulky newsrooms have become empty shells, too big to house the few remaining journalists (or content providers as we're now called).

It's all bittersweet for me. While I'm glad I work for a national publication, I do miss the give-and-take, the camaraderie I had with my fellow reporters in the newsroom. The energy and buzz of the newsroom inspired me to want to write more. Working from home, while great and convenient, can also be lonely. My only interaction with colleagues is with my editors over the phone, emails and my occasional trip to New York for meetings.

As I glide down the escalator, I recognize a small corner next to the glass windows that overlook the presses. That's where I would call Mikey during my reporting breaks to see how his day was going. Again, those Mikey and Boston memories. Arggh. I will them away. Once I reach the lobby, I swing by Terrence's desk to catch up and say goodbye before I head to a coffee shop in Dorchester to transcribe my notes.

It's just after 6 p.m. and I'm done with my story. I alert my editor in New York so she could read it over and then post it to our website. I close up my laptop and wrap up my electrical chord. I store my pad, pen, recorder and ear buds into my messenger bag. I take one last swig of my iced caramel coffee and I stride out of McKenna's coffee shop. But before I head to Rico and Oliver's in nearby Adams Village, I decide to take a walk through Savin Hill, the small neighborhood on a hill behind the newspaper.

As I saunter along the curved streets filled with old Victorian triple deckers and houses with white picket fences, I look up through the trees. The fading sunlight filters through their branches and leaves, creating a kaleidoscope of shadows on the pavement. Squirrels scurry up the trees and hop from branch to branch. The rowdy voices of a group of teenagers as they dribble and chase a basketball echo from the court at the center of the neighborhood, just under the granite-lined hill. Some people walk their dogs toward the park. I place my hands in my pockets, look down and smile.

I remember the times I would come here after work to hang out with Rico. He was single (and super horny) then and our Thursday nights and weekends often consisted of going to Club Café to check out the boys. If Rico hadn't hooked up on any of those outings which was rare, I would stay over so I wouldn't have to drive back to Cambridge. (Hey, that's the perk of having your best friend live behind your work!)

On Sundays, we enjoyed munching on toast, eggs and pancakes at McKenna's and reliving our previous night's adventure and gabbing about who hooked up with whom or which guys we liked.

Besides Club Café, Savin Hill was our other hangout. We engaged in snowball fights. We jogged along the sea wall across the way at the University of Massachusetts. Or we simply walked and talked. Being back in Boston is like being in a riptide of memories.

As I circle back to my VW which is parked along the narrow bridge that overlooks Interstate 93, I text Rico that I'm on my way.

He texts back, *Shit, it's about time. What were you doing, writing a book? Get your ass over here, TP!*

And with that, I laugh as I start my car and pull away from Savin Hill Drive toward Dorchester Avenue and to Adams Village.

A few minutes later, I pull into Rico and Oliver's driveway. I squeeze into a small space next to Rico's Goliath of a white truck.

Before they got married, Rico had moved into Oliver's beige triple-decker where he owns the first floor of the building. Rico was more than thrilled because he had pretty much hooked up with every hot and single guy in Savin Hill and he often bumped into them during his everyday travels which made for awkward interactions especially when he forgot their names.

His new neighborhood in Adams Village is home to more straight couples and families. So far, Rico hasn't bumped into any old tricks here.

I trek up the short set of wooden steps when the front door swings wide open.

"Tommy!" Rico shouts, moving in for a big hug that always lifts me off my feet.

"Hola Rico! So good to see you!" I pat him on the back. He invites me in and takes my messenger bag.

It's been a while since I've visited them and they've been busy redecorating. As I wipe my feet on the welcome mat, I notice one of Danny's wedding portraits framed and hanging in the foyer. It's the one of Rico and Oliver in their suits standing face to face holding hands.

Deeper inside the condo, the living room has what looks to be a new blue sofa and a wooden coffee table. I recognize a worn out beige love-seat that Rico had in his previous studio.

"Oliver is working late but he says hello to his favorite journalist. Wanna drink, Tommy?"

I nod as I plop myself on the sofa which absorbs my body like a soft suction.

"I want a –"

"You don't have to tell me, Tommy. I know you better than you know yourself. Vodka with diet Coke!"

"Yeah, something like that!" I wink at him.

Rico disappears into the kitchen and I hear him gather glasses and ice. I lay back on the sofa and smell the mix of old wood and orange-scented potpourri (most likely Oliver's touch.) Lining the shelves over the TV, more framed photographs of Rico and Oliver and their various adventures in white-water rafting, hiking and cycling in Provincetown. The photos show how far Rico has come in a mature relationship and how much this really feels like a true home.

"And here you go!" Rico returns with my drink and a beer for himself. He sits next to me on the sofa. We clink our glasses.

"To Dorchester and having you back in Boston, even if it's only for a few hours!" Rico holds up his beer bottle.

"And to *old* friends!" I toast back.

"Who you calling old? If I remember correctly, you're much older than me at least by eight years. Hmmm mmm." Rico lifts up his right eyebrow, smirks and looks away, waiting for my comeback. He takes a sip of his beer.

"Um, you must be getting old Rico because your memory is all foggy. You're confused. I'm 11 months older than you."

I squint at him and stick out my tongue.

He narrows his eyes back at me. We bust out laughing like the two silly friends we have always been.

"So what do you say after we have our drinks, I'll go shower and change and we hit Club Café, for old times sakes, Tommy! I think it'll be fun to see all the new Twinks at the bar and we can make fun of all the old guys there."

"Like us? Sure, it's been a while and we haven't hung out there since you went off the market. You can show off your ring whenever a young guy hits on you."

Speaking of rings, Rico holds his up to his face and poses.

"Does it bring out the hazel in my eyes?" he teases, widening and blinking his eyes.

"A little but it really brings out those huge laugh lines around your eyes!" I blurt out. To which, Rico playfully punches me, which always hurts because he sometimes forgets how strong he really is.

"So if we go, we're going in my fucking truck. Your Beetle is super gay, too gay. It looks like something that a Hello Kitty cartoon spit out. I can't be seen in it. It may ruin my reputation as a butch Italian guy, you know the one and only Italian Stallion."

"Too late. Everyone knows you're a big hungry bottom! That's why you had to move from Bottom Hill. I mean, Savin Hill!" I laugh at my cheesy zinger. Rico feigns offense.

"Um Tommy, it takes one to know one!" Rico fires back with a cocked eyebrow.

I roll my eyes at my friend.

"What am I going to do with you, Rico Suave?"

"You're stuck with me, FOR LIFE OLD MAN! We're the future *Golden Girls* of Boston. Oliver and I will always have a room for you in our home."

He punches my arm again.

"Ouch!" I whine, rubbing my arm.

It's good to be back in Boston with my best friend even if I may leave a little sore from all his playful punching.

After Rico finishes his beer, he finally takes a shower and gets ready for our boys night out. As I pass the time watching *Chronicle* on Channel 5, I wonder who we'll see at Club SoGay tonight.

18

"THIS PLACE NEVER changes, Tommy," Rico says as soon as we walk into Club Café.

"Then why are we here again? Oh, I know, because a certain Italian Stallion wanted some attention from some young guys. Hmmm mmm," I say with sass.

Rico playfully punches my shoulder which knocks me to the side and makes me laugh.

"Admit it, you do too! We might as well enjoy what little attention we can get as we slowly turn into grumpy old men, Tommy!"

I squeeze my old friend on his left shoulder as we venture deeper in this restaurant/bar/club and tourist-bathroom stop. We pass the patch of bar tables in the midsection of the wood-paneled establishment.

The throbbing pop dance music reverberates throughout the entire place and commands my feet to step to the beat. Guys mostly in their 20s and early 30s with their perfectly coiffed hair and preppy clothes lean against the bar and each other while using thin red straws to soak up their colorful cocktails.

When we arrive at the back of the bar, home to a makeshift dance floor, some guys bounce and groove in sync to Rihanna and then an

Adele remix. I bop along as I step behind Rico who shoves his way through the throngs of guys to the side bar.

A wrinkled and buffed bald bartender who has been here just as long as Rico and I have lived in Boston - or longer - greets us with a friendly smile.

"Hey, I haven't seen you two in a looong time. Where have you guys been hiding?"

"Well, this one over here got hitched and is living the married life," I explain.

Rico proudly flashes his ring and then curls his bicep. I shake my head left and right, roll my eyes and continue talking.

"And I moved to Maine. Ogunquit to be exact."

"Well, welcome back! Let me guess, a vodka with Diet Coke, right? And your buddy there likes light beer."

Rico and I look at one another. We raise our eyebrows and nod our heads.

"YES!" we declare at the same time.

"Coming right up!" the bartender says as he starts to make my drink.

While we wait, Rico and I turn around and study the scene before us. Twinks flirt with one another, some making out in the corner and on the dance floor while Twerking or bopping to the music. Older men in their 50s with more salt than pepper in their hair stand sentinel on the outskirts of the dance floor watching everything unfold.

And then there's Rico and me, looking around and then looking at each other and grinning, indulging on those-were-the-days.

"Remember how we came here every single Thursday night for years, Tommy?"

"Good times, Rico. Good times. We were Club Café those days!" I reminisce.

The bartender returns with our drinks and plops them on the polished wooden counter.

I fumble for some dollar bills from my wallet when the bartender shoos my hand away.

"These are on me. Now don't be strangers. Got it?"

I smile and nod.   Rico holds up his light beer to my glass.

"To Club Café!" I toast.

"To Tommy!"

"To Rico!"

"To...Mikey?" Rico says, looking past my shoulder.

"Mikey? Huh? What are you talking about?" I twist my nose, feeling suddenly confused. Rico nods his chin up for me to look behind me.

I slowly turn around and the picture slowly comes into focus. The light blue eyes. The sandy brown straight hair. The smattering of facial scruff. The sweet smile.

My ex. My heart hammers inside my chest. My pulse quickens.

I'm paralyzed for a moment. I don't even hear the music anymore. It's just me staring at my first love. A lump forms in my throat. Words fail me.

"Don't just stand there. Say Hi. Stop being a fucking dweeb!" Rico says, shoving me.

I stumble and almost fall on Mikey. My drink splashes on my hand. I try to wipe it dry with the side of my pants. And I suddenly hear the music again as if an inner switch turned it back on. And I quickly regain my composure.

"Hey Tommy, how have you been? It's, um, been a while," Mikey says with his endearing Boston accent which makes my name sound like Tah-mie.

"Sorry, Mikey. I didn't mean to be rude. You just caught me by surprise."

He moves in for a hug and we awkwardly embrace. In the second or two that passes, I inhale his citrusy cologne and his mint gum. It all feels so familiar again. My emotions are scattered right now, sadness mingled with joy. I'm not sure which one dominates over the other right now.

"Guys, I need to go to the little boy's room. I'll be back in a bit," Rico announces with a devilish grin, his hazel eyes twinkle mischief. He's enjoying watching me squirm and melt over seeing Mikey again.

As Rico puffs out his chest and stomps away, he makes a silly face that only I could see.

I playfully narrow my eyes at him.

Now it's just Mikey and me, standing face to face trying to make small talk. I glance down and notice that he's drinking a bottle of water. He doesn't seem drunk at all like the other times we hung out at Club Cafe. In fact, he's quite lucid and focused, on me.

"I heard you moved to Maine. I haven't seen you in ages, Tommy Boy!" he says, calling me by my old nickname.

I quickly tell him about my apartment in Ogunquit and working for *People*.

"I know! My grandma sees your byline in the magazine. She's a subscriber. She needs her *People* every Friday to take to the senior center. It sounds like you're doing well, Tommy. I'm happy for you." He looks at me and looks away.

I grin and take a swig of my drink. A stream of guys passes us to and from the bar leaving a mix of powdery and grassy colognes in their heady wake.

"Thank you. I really like living in Maine. It's slower and quiet. I feel really at peace there. I read a lot and hike on the weekends when I can."

"I remember how much you liked the Blue Hills. We used to go together, remember?"

He playfully bites down on his tongue. I nod.

"Do you still have that funny looking Volkswagen? It looked like a giant tomato or something."

I grin at the comparison.

"Of course, I do. I could never part with my Bug. It's cute and unique."

"Just like you, Tommy."

I awkwardly smile as I look down at my drink. The more we talk, the more my stomach cramps up, stabbing me with pangs of guilt. Like a photo gallery in my mind, images of Ignacio unfold one after the other. One is of him surprising me with the welcome-back-home balloons. Another image of him holding up Amiga as they knock (or scratch in her case) at my front door. I then see him serving me the delicious flan he whipped up during one of our dates. This encounter with Mikey doesn't feel right even though it was by chance.

"Tommy, are you still there? Hello! I think you just went off somewhere in your head, like you used to." Mikey winks.

"Sorry about that. I was just thinking about Maine. I'm seeing someone there," I explain nonchalantly.

Mikey tilts his head to the right and slightly pouts.

"Of course you are. Who wouldn't want to date a handsome writer? You were always solid as a rock. Mr. Responsible and Dependable. I figured you wouldn't be single for too long after we… you know." He doesn't finish the thought but I know what he meant to say, since our break up.

"Thanks. How about you?" I place my drink back down on the counter out of Mikey's sight like I used to whenever we went out. I wouldn't want Mikey to feel tempted or uncomfortable watching me drink even though he is in a gay bar.

"I've seen some guys here and there. It's hard dating in Boston. Everybody knows everybody and everybody knows each other's business. Most of the guys I've met like to drink a lot and that's not good for me to be around. So I rather be single for the time being."

I pat him on the shoulder.

"That is really good to hear, Mikey. It looks like you're still sober."

"I am. I've been sober since we went our separate ways. I go to meetings twice a week but I still like to socialize. I'm here with the guys from the basketball league. We stop by once a week after practice. And this is my drink of choice."

He proudly holds up his bottle of water. He grins and playfully bites down on his tongue.

We stand and stare and smile for a minute and then two. No words are exchanged.

A sadness washes over me as I look at this sweet beautiful man who resided in a big part of my heart. And perhaps he still does in a way.

"Yo Mikey, we're ready to order. Are you coming?" a tall lean guy in a blue basketball jersey shouts from the end of the bar.

"The guys are waiting!" the guy shouts.

Mikey tells him that he'll be right there.

"Tommy, I wish I could talk some more but I gotta get back to the team. We're celebrating one of the guy's birthdays," he says but his eyes betray him, revealing an inner truer desire to stay with me for a while longer.

"I totally understand. Go be with your teammates. It was good seeing you."

"Ditto Tommy! Ditto!" Mikey moves in for hug and we embrace tightly, as if for the last time.

As he walks away, I grab my drink and drain it. I exhale loudly. This is one of the reasons why I moved away, to avoid these accidental encounters with Mikey. They are emotional twisters that I rather dodge.

I look ahead and Rico finally reappears, walking with his signature gusto. He looks at Mikey who is walking away toward the restaurant. Rico smirks at me.

"What did I miss? You guys look like you stepped in shit or came from a funeral."

"In a way, we did. I think I was saying goodbye to Mikey for the last time. I don't want to come back here anymore."

Rico squeezes my upper right shoulder to comfort me like he used to whenever I had a problem with Mikey's excessive drinking.

"For what it's worth, I think it was good that you saw him. You needed to finally close that book once and for all. And now you can move forward with Mr. Mexico!' Rico says with mischief.

"Um, Costa Rica, Rico. Get your countries straight."

"Same thing,'' he jokes, playfully punching me in the shoulder which at this point, is permanently black and blue.

"Now will you order me another beer? This one's on you, Tommy. Like the good old days!"

We turn around, squeeze among the young guys at the bar and hail the bartender once again, like old times.

19

IT'S ANOTHER BEAUTIFUL day in Maine. The sun is shining. The ocean glistens and I'm on all fours looking for my organizer.

It's Sunday morning and I'm home preparing for my week of stories and interviews. But first, my organizer. I looked in my messenger bag and my desk. No luck. I scratch the side of my head as I stand in my bedroom and rummage through my desk some more. The sun floods through my window, highlighting the patches of color of my comforter and the beige carpeting.

I search under the bed. Still, no luck. Where could I have left it? Perhaps at the newspaper the other day or at Rico's the other night? I crawl around my bedroom like a playful giant when I suddenly hear some frantic scratching and whimpering at my front door. What can that be now?

I get up and amble to the door. When I open it, I look down and see Amiga, trembling as if she emerged from a frozen lake. She jumps toward my knees. She looks scared. I squat down and pet her.

"Hey, hey…it's okay. Where is Ignacio? What are you doing all alone?" I ask Amiga as if she could answer my questions.

She climbs onto my knees and nestles herself in my arms. I cradle her like a baby and rub her furry white stomach.

"Shhh…Calm down. It's okay."

As I rock her in my arms, she half-closes her eyes. She licks my right hand.

"Hey, that tickles! I don't know where that tongue has been, Amiga!"

I laugh at my own joke.

Just as I'm about to close the door, I hear Ignacio.

"Tommy, *ay dios mio*! Thank God she came here."

He rushes toward my door and comes inside. Creases form on his forehead. He's all sweaty. He immediately pets Amiga's head.

"She's okay. She's calming down. What happened, Ignacio?"

He kisses me on the lips and rubs my left arm. I close the door and we head to my living room where I carefully place Amiga on my red sofa. She wiggles her behind into a corner and settles in. She takes a deep sniff, of what, I don't know. My apartment smells like lavender, thanks to my Plug-ins.

Ignacio sits next to her and I next to him. Amiga looks up at Ignacio and then at me with her big brown eyes.

"I was by the front door of the inn, about to put on her leash when fireworks or a motorcycle engine or something loud scared her. She ran off before I could grab her. She was like a white bullet. I called out to her and chased her which made her run faster. When I saw the direction she was heading, I sensed that she might come here."

Ignacio then narrows his eyes and scolds her.

"You gave me a big scare, Amiga! Bad girl! Bad girl! No treats for you tonight," he says, pointing his index finger at her.

She rests her chin on her paws. She heaves a sigh. Really. Guilty as charged. This dog is too funny.

Then she stares my way.

"Don't look at me, Amiga. It's your dad who's mad at you. I look at her with a raised eyebrow and smirk. I cross my arms.

"In a way, this is a good sign, Tommy."

Ignacio leans back on the sofa and spreads his legs. He folds his hands and rests them on his stomach, relieved that the episode is over.

"What do you mean?" I place my hand on Ignacio's knee and squeeze.

"She came here because she trusts you. She feels safe here. This is becoming another home for her. She knew where to go when she was scared. To that, I will always be grateful to you."

I place my hand over my chest.

"Awe...Amiga! Mi one-bedroom-apartment es tu one-bedroom-apartment. And oh yeah, you too, Ignacio." I wink. She lifts up her head and barks, as if in agreement.

Ignacio then leans over and plants another kiss on my lips which I savor. I can taste the salt from his sweat.

As we kiss, Amiga leaps over us and the sofa and darts toward my bedroom. I hear her running around in circles and shaking something. What is this crazy dog doing now? At least she can't run away in here.

A few seconds later, she emerges with something in her mouth. As she comes into focus, I laugh. She found my organizer.

"What's so funny, Tommy?" I shake my head side to side. I bend down and put out my hand. Amiga places the organizer in it.

"It's a long story, Ignacio. I'm glad you guys came over."

After putting away the organizer in a place I would find it (the top of my desk next to my cell phone,) I head to the kitchen. I offer Ignacio some orange or apple juice and diet soda, the only choices in my fridge besides water. He asks for the OJ and I pour some into a glass.

I hand it him and he takes a sip. His face suddenly turns serious.

"It's good that Amiga stopped by. I need to share some news with you, Tommy."

Ignacio eyes his drink and circles the rim of his glass with his index finger. Amiga then rejoins us on the sofa where she begins to lick her private parts.

"What's going on? Is it bad?" I scoot closer to Ignacio and rub the back of his neck with my hand.

He looks up at me with his hazel orbs.

"I got a job."

"I know you have a job. So tell me what's on your mind. Why the long face?"

"No, I mean that I found a new job. I'm leaving Ogunquit. Labor Day weekend is my last weekend here."

Amiga's ears perk up like antennas when he says the word leaving.

"A new job? Oh wow. That was quick. Where? Um, that's wonderful. I know you wanted to leave before it got cold here," I say, faking my enthusiasm. I glance down at my hands.

"The job is in Fort Lauderdale. I'll be helping run a gay hotel near the beach. They offered me an assistant manager position which comes with housing in the back of the hotel. There's a dog park nearby for Amiga and I know how much she loves playing on the beach. I'll be back in South Florida and closer to my family. There are direct flights to Costa Rica from the airport in Fort Lauderdale. I couldn't say no."

My heart sinks. Deep down, I was enjoying having them in Ogunquit. They've been glimmers of happiness. They really have become a part of my life. But if this is what Ignacio wants, I have to be happy for him and not be a selfish jerk. What choice do I have?

I understand, or understood, the pull of family and the seductive warm weather of South Florida. I've gotten used to being alone in Ogunquit. It will be okay. I'll have to go back to the way things were pre-Ignacio and post-Mikey. The single life seems to be a permanent condition for me. Work always keeps me busy anyway. I do my best to stamp out my inner sadness and to be happy for this great guy despite feeling strangely bothered by the news.

I reach over and hug him, rubbing his upper back.

"I'm happy for you, if this is what you want. I can just imagine Amiga trotting along Fort Lauderdale beach and flirting with all the other terriers and poodles." I also imagine the muscular Fort Lauderdale queens hitting on Ignacio. My stomach begins to cramp from jealousy.

I lean my head on his forehead and I kiss him. I entwine my fingers with his.

"We still have another month before I leave, Tommy. I want to make the best of our time together. And now you'll have two reasons to visit Fort Lauderdale."

Ignacio smiles and I half-grin back.

Again, Amiga playfully barks.

"I think she agrees," Ignacio says as Amiga wiggles in between us on the sofa and licks both of us.

20

"HEY BEST MAN! Are you in Ogunquit?" Danny says on the other line.

"Hey Danny. Good to hear from you. Yeah, I'm working from home as usual. What's up?"

"I'm shooting Randy Price and his husband for a feature in *Boston Spirit* magazine. They live in Kittery, not far from you. Wanna meet up for coffee or lunch later?"

"Sure, I could use a caffeine fix or a cookie break," I say, giving him my address.

"I'll text you when I'm on my way, BEST MAN!"

"Okay, see you then."

I press END on my phone and place it on top of my desk. I then return to preparing some notes and background for my story. It's about a wealthy New Hampshire couple who cloned their Labrador. They spent $150,000 working with a lab in Korea to make a copy of their beloved Max which died of cancer a year ago.

The couple froze his DNA when they learned about the cloning science. And now they have a sugar-colored puppy named Dax that looks and supposedly acts just like Max. I already interviewed them on the phone for some background and I'm meeting them tomorrow morning at their estate for some color. The cloned pooch is something I need to see with my own eyes.

I confirm the time of the interview in my organizer, which sits at my desk right where I can see it. As I stretch my arms upward and yawn, I think of Danny and his assignment today. Hmmm, Randy Price. Why does that name sound so familiar? Oh, that's the morning TV news anchor from Boston. He was the first openly gay TV news anchor in the country. I met him a few times during my Boston media gatherings and once at Club Café where he headlined a fundraiser for local pet rescues. He looks like a grey-haired version of the Ron Burgundy character from those silly Will Ferrell *Anchorman* movies.

As my fingers continue tapping on my laptop, my thoughts drift back to Ignacio. Where will things stand a month from now when he's in Fort Lauderdale? I suppose we can keep in touch but dating will be a challenge. I live in the northernmost state of the East Coast and he'll be in the southernmost.

We could Skype and Facetime but it won't be the same. Now we can easily walk to and from each other's homes. And then there is Amiga. I know I'm going to miss that little white dog with the funny black markings. I push the thoughts aside to focus on my story at hand. I still have some quality time left with Ignacio and Amiga. I need to make the most of it.

Two hours later, Danny texts me that he's on his way. I save my work files and close my laptop. Once again, I stand up and stretch and exhale loudly. I use the back of an old *People* magazine to brush up the white dog hairs from my sofa. I try to tidy up the living room by rearranging the pillows into a neat order.

While I wait for Danny, I plop myself on the sofa and I tune into NECN to see what's happening around the region. The sunlight warms my face.

About 20 minutes later, I hear three consecutive knocks on my front door. When I open the door, Danny appears with a big smile which seems whiter thanks to his sun-baked skin.

He's wearing a loose white button down shirt, faded blue jeans and sneakers.

"It's Maine's BEST MAN! So good to see you, Tommy."

He envelopes me into a big hug, similar to Rico's. I immediately catch a whiff of his sporty after shave.

I pat him on the upper back.

"Welcome to Ogunquit! I see you still have some of your Key West coloring."

"Why thank you! I was going for that Miami Latino look, the caramel skin. *Te gusta*?" he says playfully. He places his hands on his waist like a super hero and poses to the side.

"It agrees with you. You have a few weeks of warm weather to work on it some more." I wouldn't say that Danny was super tanned. He's like a human version of white bread that has been lightly toasted.

"So where are we going, Tommy? This is your hood."

"I know this cute little coffee place in town. Anyone who is a who's-who especially a gay who's who goes there."

"So I guess you don't go there a lot?" Danny teases, with a wink.

I purse my lips and feign offense.

"On second thought, I have a lot of work to finish…"

"Okay, I was kidding BEST MAN! You're definitely a who's who in Ogunquit. In Maine, in New England for that matter."

"Now that's more like it. We can walk there so let's go!" I lock my front door and lead the way onto Route One.

At the Backyard coffeehouse, the succulent aroma of baked goods and fresh coffee greet us as I order an espresso while Danny asks for a chamomile tea at the front counter. Customers, a mix of tourists and locals mostly in shorts, tank tops and sandals, linger inside sipping their drinks as they enjoy a cool respite from the summer heat.

With our drinks in hand, we sit in a corner table for two by the glass windows that face the huge lot where everyone parks when visiting Ogunquit for the day.

I ask him about his photo shoot with Randy Price and his husband.

"It went really well. They have this sprawling house on a cliff that overlooks the ocean. We shot some photos in their garden and some with their dogs. Can you believe these guys have a custom built kennel under their house? They have about 10 dogs. The story is about their prize-winning dogs. This is for the fall issue of the magazine."

"I'll definitely check it out, Danny."

I sprinkle some sugar into my coffee.

"So what's new with BEST MAN! I talked to Rico the other day and he said you guys hung out in Boston."

"Yeah, we went to our old stomping ground. I think we were the oldest guys at the bar. I'm glad those barhopping days are over. It's too much work. I would rather stay home or meet up with friends at a restaurant."

"Or a coffeehouse!" Danny interrupts holding up his cup of tea.

"It's funny that you mention your story on the couple's dogs. I've been thinking that I should get one myself. I'm home a lot and I could use the company.

I really don't have many friends nearby. I could use a fur buddy."

"Does this have anything to do with the white little dog that you've posted photos of on Instagram?"

I flash Danny a big smile.

"Oh, that's Amiga, Ignacio's dog. I've become kind of attached to her. They dropped by yesterday."

"I can tell," Danny says, leaning over. He then plucks a strand of white dog hair from my black T-shirt. He holds it up with his finger.

"Yeah, she sheds. I need to vacuum my place. Speaking of, I won't be seeing much more of her soon."

Danny leans in closer and takes a sip of his tea.

"How come?"

"Ignacio landed a job in Fort Lauderdale. They're moving down before Labor Day."

I glance down at my steaming espresso.

"You really like him, don't you, Tommy?"

"I think it's a little more than like," I say wistfully.

I rest my chin on my right hand and stare out the window.

"I think it's sweet you met a guy that you more than like. My advice, if you want it, is to see how things go. Don't put any pressure on yourself or him. Enjoy your time together and see what happens. Let life surprise you. If it's meant to be, things will work out. Who knows, you may get an assignment or two down in Miami. Then you can see Ignacio and what's her name again?"

"Amiga! Thanks for the advice. Things just feel so up in the air," I say, holding up my hands.

"The one thing that I've learned from losing Rick so suddenly is don't take things for granted. Appreciate the moments. Make the most out of life because you never know what will happen tomorrow. No regrets, BEST MAN!"

Danny holds up his right fist and bumps mine.

"Say it with me. NO REGRETS, BEST MAN!"

"NO REGRETS BEST MAN!" I repeat after him which makes Danny shake his head side to side and roll his eyes.

We may have said it too loudly because a pack of customers in line turns around and looks at us quizzically as if we were aliens.

"What am I going to do with you, BEST MAN!"

"You can start by getting me another espresso and a chocolate chip cookie." I tease him.

"Hey, that might be a good name for your future dog."

"Espresso?" I say, furrowing my eyebrows.

"No, I meant Cookie. That's what you can name your dog."

After Danny returns with another cup of espresso and a cookie for moi, he settles back into his chair across from me.

"So besides photographing Mr. Boston TV, what's new with you, Danny?"

He leans back and rests his hands on his flat stomach.

"The assignments have been steady so I can't complain. They've been keeping me busy. A mix of online, magazine and newspaper assignments. But I have one assignment in particular that I was thinking that I could use your help with."

"I don't think I would make a good camera assistant, if that's what you're talking about. And I really don't have time to take on any more assignments."

"Nah, it's nothing like that, BEST MAN!" he says, taking another slurp of his tea.

I'm intrigued. What does Danny need my help with?

"This is for another assignment for *Boston Spirit*. They are doing a story on a gay wedding boutique. I'm shooting the owner but I need a model, a guy to wear some of the suits for a shoot. The store owner said he wanted a guy with nice dark curly hair and a friendly easygoing smile to pose in his suits. Someone local that people can relate to. I happened to show him some shots from Carlos's wedding."

"And did I mention that we're on a budget or lack thereof...." Danny says, trailing off, his eyes widening.

"Danny, I don't know anyone like that, except may be Carlos but his hair has been short since the wedding but I don't think he'd want to do this anyway. He can be shy sometimes."

Danny exhales loudly in frustration. He folds his arms.

"No, Captain Oblivious. I was talking about you. You fit the profile."

"Me? Huh? I think I am going to start call you loco, too! Did they put something in your tea to come up with this crazy idea? I'm not a model."

"Yes, you, BEST MAN! It wouldn't take more than an hour next weekend. I can't pay you but I can treat you to lunch or dinner wherever you want, even TGIFriday's. Carlos said that was your favorite place. And you'll have some great photos to share with your friends and family or even Ignacio."

I'm flattered, touched really. Danny probably has a network of models to choose from and he came, to me? The idea tickles my ego, just a little. I'm not a model, not even close but Danny thinks that I could pull this off somehow. The more I think about it, the more I look forward to the shoot and helping Danny. I think everybody should feel like a model at least once in their life. And why not at 40? I'm not getting younger. The shoot would also serve as a good distraction from Ignacio's pending move south. And I could use the distraction.

As I start thinking about the possible suits and ties and posing to the left and right like a contestant on *Next Top Groom*, I suddenly start to giggle which makes Danny laugh.

"What's so funny?" he says.

"I was just thinking that it's a little ironic that I've never been proposed to but I get to be a groom, at least for one afternoon. I'd be happy to help you out. At least I can see how it finally feels like to dress up like the man of the hour."

"You're going to do great. I wouldn't have asked if I didn't think so. Thanks for agreeing to help me out." Danny says, extending his right hand and patting mine.

"Hey, anything for a friend."

"Consider this practice for when your big day at the altar comes, BEST MAN!"

I smile at the idea but the way things are going in my love life, the altar seems like a mirage in the desert, something to aspire to but never reach.

21

IT'S JUST PAST 3 p.m. and I'm back in Boston on this sun dappled Sunday afternoon. I'm standing a few feet away from Danny as he shoots photos of me for the gay wedding boutique which sits on the ground level of a red-brick brownstone in the South End.

We're inside the shop which is closed for the afternoon so that he could snap some photos without being interrupted by onlookers.

"Okay, BEST MAN! Now turn your face slightly to the left. Hold your pose... perfect! Now turn slightly to the right for a few more shots," Danny instructs.

I tilt my head to the right. I slip my hands into the front pockets of the suit's black pants.

Now I know why he really wanted me to model these suits – to boss me around. I give him my best withering look.

"Now you look constipated. Give me one of your big smiles. There you go. YES! YES! Just like that. You're getting the hang of this. Just remember to have fun, BEST MAN."

"I'm doing my best, Danny," I say through clenched teeth. I play with the red necktie and playfully glance up.

"No, not like that. That's too playful. Stick to the smile or slight grin and we'll be done before you know it. You have another suit to try on after this one."

I stick out my tongue like an obnoxious kid.

"Do you think the boutique owner would like that shot?" I tease.

"Um, no. Well, maybe. You never know. He does like guys with curly hair. Okay, now we need a profile shot by the window where the light can better bounce off the suit."

Danny motions for me to stand by the boutique's front window. It faces rows of shoulder-to-shoulder brick brownstones anchored by shops, cafes and convenient stores on the first floor.

"Now pretend some hot guy said something really flattering to you and you're feeling all-you know-chucks, bashful. Yes, that's the look. And I want you to glance down and then up again as if you're seeing that hot guy walk by the shop."

"I like how you add a back story to the photo. This makes it easier to relate to," I turn to Danny whose camera clicks clicks clicks after each shot.

"I think you're really liking this imaginary hot guy, Tommy because you're blushing. A LOT. Your cheeks are rosy which compliments the tie. And who are you thinking about?"

I smile and look down. Heat flushes my cheeks.

"Ignacio."

"Well, keep thinking about him. Your face is lighting up like a Christmas tree." Danny's camera continues to click away. Then he points the camera down away from his torso and studies some of the images that he took.

"Want to take a look? I got some good shots. I think we're ready for the other suit."

I walk over and browse the gallery of images. I laugh when I see the one where I'm sticking out my tongue.

"I think you should go with that one for the magazine, for sure. If not, I'll post it on my Instagram."

Danny purses his lips and shakes his head side to side.

"I'm glad I'm the one who picks the winning photo and trust me, that ain't it. Anyway, go change into the gray suit but use the same tie. And before I forget, the owner of the shop said you could have the red necktie as a gift for being such a good sport. He has one in a box with your name on it by the register."

"Oh wow. That's so sweet, Danny. I'll have to write him a thank you note." I shuffle to the register where I find the gift box.

My fingers graze the plastic see-through cover and I smile as I marvel the tie. This makes my sixth necktie. I'm adding it to my collection of ties from all the weddings I've been to in recent years. But I plan to save this one for a special event. The red really pops.

A few minutes later, I step out of the dressing room wearing the other suit but with the same tie. Danny positions me by the window. I repeat the same poses.

"Keep thinking about Ignacio, BEST MAN. Your blushing again. Yes! Now look away from the camera and then smile as you look straight at me. Yes. W*ork, work, work work, work*, like that Rihanna song."

I place my hands along the suit's vest and I pose from each side.

"So things must be going well with Ignacio for him to make you glow like Rudolf," Danny says, his face obscured by the camera. All I see is his black wavy hair above the rim of the camera.

"Things have been great. A little too great, for now."

Danny puts his camera down. His eyes widen. His thin black eyebrows arch.

"Have you given more thought about what you guys are going to do when he moves?"

"That's the thing. I don't know. I'm taking your advice from the other day to go with the flow and not have any regrets but how is that going to work when he's flowing in Fort Lauderdale and I'll be flowing in Maine."

"Maybe you can talk to him about having a long-distance relationship? Hey, it works, sometimes. You never know until you try. Or you can just accept things for what they are. You had a great summer together and that might be it. Just go into this with your eyes open, that's all, so you know what you're getting yourself into."

I would hate to think of it that way. Just a summer fling.

"I don't mean to be nosy BEST MAN but have you told him how you feel, whatever way you're leaning?"

"I haven't yet. I know what I want to say but..." I trail off.

"It needs to come from your heart, BEST MAN. You'll know when the time is right."

"I'm planning to surprise him with a little road trip to Rhode Island next week so maybe then." I smile sheepishly.

"Well, in the meantime, let's focus on these suits. Now let's take some photos outside. We have perfect natural soft light. The side of the building is a red-bricked wall. That will nicely contrast with the gray suit and compliment the red from the tie - and your cheeks!"

Danny opens the front door of the shop and I follow him outside. We walk to the corner of the block where he positions me against the bare brick wall.

He moves a few feet back and starts shooting again.

"Keep thinking about how Ignacio makes you feel. Yes, just like that. Make those cheeks glow, BEST MAN!"

I smile broadly. I laugh as I model from each side. Some people walk by and stare which makes me look away, embarrassed.

As Danny shoots, I finger the soft tie. My thoughts drift to Ignacio's stunning eyes, his soft warm kisses and those magical words I want to tell him soon.

22

"**WHERE ARE WE** going, Tommy?" Ignacio asks, climbing inside my Volkswagen. Amiga hops in too and settles at his feet.

"It's a surprise. *Shh*!" I hold up my finger to my lips. I playfully wiggle my eyebrows.

"But where is the surprise? "

He fastens his seat belt and clicks it into place.

"Ignacio, it wouldn't be a surprise if I told you. Humor me, por favor. It's a fun day trip. Don't worry. We're staying in New England. I want to show you one of my favorite cities. I never get down there enough and I wanted to share it with you."

He smiles as he leans over and plops a sweet kiss on my lips. I squeeze his left knee.

"Thank you, Tommy. Did you hear that Amiga? Tommy is taking us on a little trip." Amiga's ears perk up. She then leaps onto his lap and looks at me.

I grin at them as I put on my sunglasses and turn the ignition.

"And we're off to Destination Unknown!" I say, pulling out of my driveway toward Route 1.

As we drive on I-95 south toward Massachusetts, Ignacio rhythmically combs Amiga's fur with his fingers. Her eyes are half closed.

She's in heaven. Every now and then, Ignacio looks out from his passenger window which unfolds in various shades of greens from the roadside trees. I lower the volume from the country music station.

"Hey, so are you all set for your move to Fort Lauderdale?" I ask Ignacio who turns away from the window and toward me.

"I haven't started packing or anything. I don't have a lot of stuff. I am going to ship some boxes ahead so that when I fly down, I'll only have a suitcase, a bag, and a carrier for Amiga. That's the advantage of living in a hotel room. You live like a minimalist. You only have what you really need."

As he speaks, Amiga looks at up him as though she understands everything he says.

"If I didn't say this before, I want you to know that I think this is a great opportunity for you and Amiga. I'm not going to lie. I am definitely going to miss you two. You helped make Ogunquit feel more like a home in such a short period of time."

Ignacio's eyes brighten. A slight smile forms on his lips. He takes his left hand and slips it into my right hand and squeezes. He reaches over and kisses my cheek.

"You also helped make Ogunquit feel like home too, Tommy."

He then starts to rub the back of my head. I push my neck deeper into the palm of his hand. No matter where or how he touches me, it feels sensual, so good, like tiny waves of electricity swarming my body. I am definitely going to miss that.

I begin to get a little too excited in my shorts, which forces me to shift in my seat.

"Okay, I need to focus. We have another hour or so to go. We can play later on tonight."

"Now I'm excited, Tommy Perez. Focus on the road. I think I'm going to take a little nap," Ignacio says, as he pulls the right lever on the passenger seat to lay down.

Amiga climbs over him and curls up on the seat behind mine.

"Sweet dreams!" I say, as I navigate the Beetle. We pass the big green and white signs for Danvers, Boston and then Waltham. But I keep heading south.

It's just shy of 1 p.m. The sun glazes the curving snake-like Interstate 95. We drive by several old triple decker homes and historic churches that overlook the highway.

With my index finger, I gently poke Ignacio in his stomach.

"Wake up! We're here."

He opens his eyes and rubs them with his knuckles. He yawns and stretches his arms.

He glances out the passenger window and reads the sign that states "Welcome to Rhode Island, the Ocean State."

"Ah, we must be going to Providence, right?"

I grin and nod in agreement.

"Oh wow. I've never been there. I don't get to travel much because of work. Thank you Tommy for bringing us here."

"No problem. It's another slice of New England. I used to come here all the time when I lived in Boston. It was a little weekend get-away. "

As I drive, the white statehouse comes into focus on our left. Not far behind it is the red-bricked Biltmore Hotel and the small patch of skyscrapers that dwarf the city. Providence Place Mall beckons ahead with its parking garage that fronts the highway.

I slow down as I pull off exit 22C. We make our way into the down-town area where the buildings wear various shades of brick, from red to brown.

A few minutes later, I parallel park my car near the train station. It sits in front of the statehouse which reminds me of a cake topper for a wedding. The three of us hop out of my car and Ignacio immediately places a leash on Amiga. Her small little black tail wags happily left and right. I feed a few quarters into the parking meter.

We trek toward the river just below the mall. Many tourists and locals look over the railings at the slow-moving sheet of water below. Patches of sunlight highlight the swarms of fish roaming the river.

Ignacio takes it all in. He cranes his neck toward the towering pink and beige residential buildings with their glass balconies. We stroll toward the collection of vintage brick buildings that lead up the hill toward the Rhode Island School of Design and Brown University. The city teems with pedestrian life. Teen boys with shoulder-length curly or straight hair skateboard along the river's walkway. Couples ride their bicycles. Some folks walk their dogs. Cars and buses zip along Memorial Boulevard, the wide road that cuts through the city.

"It's like a mini-Boston but with better parking," I joke as we reach the bottom of a steep incline toward the colleges.

"This is so charming, Tommy. I think it's prettier than Boston," Ignacio says with a grin. We begin to walk up the street and Amiga pulls ahead seemingly leading the way.

"I totally agree. It's more manageable. You can have a better quality of life here than in Boston where things have become too expensive. The streets are wider in Providence and I happen to think the people are nicer too. But that's just me."

I smile at Ignacio.

Once we reach the entrance of Brown University, I point to the school's courtyard dotted with thick leafy trees that line the walkways. Students in shorts and T-shirts trek from building to building.

Two young guys toss a Frisbee on one of the lawns. Side by side, Ignacio and I sit at one of the nearby metallic benches. Amiga jumps on my lap and kisses my chin.

"You're so sweet, Amiga. I love you!"

I toss my head back and giggle from all her wet sloppy kisses.

"She loves you too, Tommy."

Ignacio settles his arm behind my back. He looks longingly at me with his stunning hazel eyes. He takes a deep breath.

"And Tommy...I love you, too."

The declaration catches me off guard. I remove my sunglasses. My eyes widen. Heat rises into my cheeks.

"I...I..." I stammer, at a loss for words.

He moves in for a kiss before I can fully respond. He softly kisses me, brushing his lips against mine. I cup the back of his neck with my right hand and squeeze. A soft breeze blows through the courtyard and through my hair.

When I gently pull back from the kiss, Ignacio whispers.

"You don't have to say anything. I wanted you to know how I feel, how I have felt for a while now."

"I'm, um, speechless," I say, searching for the right words to say but nothing seems to be coming out.

"Shhh...Tommy. It's okay. I didn't tell you that so that you can tell me the same thing. When the time is right, you can tell me how you really feel about me."

I avert my gaze and look down at Amiga. I take advantage of his kind offer – deferring my feelings. Where did this guy come from? He's handsome, sweet, caring. Being with him feels so natural, so good. So why can't I just say...*it!* Why am I holding back? Amiga looks up at me with her big brown eyes as if telling me through telepathy, *Tommy, don't be a dork. Tell him how you feel too.*

I look back at her and silently respond *I will....I promise...Just not now. Now go back to licking your private parts.*

I think Amiga heard me because she does exactly that. I smile to myself.

"Now that you've seen a little bit of Brown, let's keep walking. There is a cute street nearby with coffee shops and dog-friendly restaurants. We can grab lunch there."

"Let's go!" Ignacio says, wrapping Amiga's leash around his hand. She leaps off his lap and onto the ground.

Ignacio and I get up from the bench and follow some students toward Thayer Street, a bustling one-way thoroughfare of boutiques, clothing stores and the Brown bookstore.

As we pass the university's black gates and stride along the paved sidewalk, another cool breeze greets us. Ignacio looks at me and smiles. We don't have many afternoons like this left in New England and I feel my inner clock ticking loudly. I look up at the bright blue sky and mentally thank and curse Cupid for sending me a great guy but at the wrong time. What's the point of saying how I really feel when he's moving away in a few weeks?

After having a fat turkey sandwich and a burger at a cafe off Thayer Street, I stroll with Ignacio and Amiga along Angell Street to Wayland Square. We grab some coffee at the Starbucks and sit outside under the afternoon light. Every few minutes, a cool breeze passes through, another reminder that summer will end soon.

A wooden fence lined with bushes ribbons the perimeter of the coffeehouse's patio. College students with their laptops plop down at the black metal tables near us. Two elderly residents open up the Providence newspaper as they sip their lattes and tea. Up and down Angell, people ride their bicycles and walk their dogs along the beige and gray-colored clapboard homes and triple-decker residences.

I lean back in my chair, my legs crossed and arms dangling to my sides. Amiga's warm body rests on my feet. Her ears perk up whenever a dog passes by.

"What is this area, Tommy?"

"It's Wayland Square, a mix of students, families and young professionals. We're right in the heart of it. You pretty much have everything here. Coffee shop, a bookstore, boutiques. There's a Whole Foods a few blocks away and a gym. This is very neighborhoody.

You're in the city but it feels more like a little suburb," I say, holding my cup of double espresso and blowing on the rim. Steam rises.

"It's very cute. Right, Amiga?" Ignacio says. Amiga playfully barks backs. Ignacio twirls a straw in his caramel iced coffee. The dog gladly licks the bottom of the plastic cup.

"Probably the closest thing to this neighborhood in Fort Lauderdale is Wilton Manors but with more gay men. Lots of them. It's like a gay retirement village. When you drive through Wilton Manors, a giant rainbow forms over the city and you suddenly hear Broadway musicals." I grin at my cheesy joke.

Ignacio's eyes crinkle.

"You know, Tommy, I'm going to miss it up here, especially Ogunquit. It's a charming little town. Amiga and I have been very happy there. She loves her walks along Marginal Way."

"It's grown on me, too. At first, I missed everything about Boston, running along the Charles River, going out in the South End, seeing Carlos and Rico all the time and any time I wanted. But the more time I spent in Ogunquit, the easier and simpler my life became. I felt this calm, this peacefulness that I had lost in Boston with constantly going out to Club Café and hanging out in the South End. I think that's why I was so drawn to Providence too. You can have a nice quality of life here as in Ogunquit. It's just... a different rhythm, you know. "

"If you ever need to get away from the cold, come down and stay with us in Fort Lauderdale. We can go to Wilton Manors and see that giant rainbow over the city you told me about and maybe listen to those Broadway musicals."

"I always visit Miami during the winter, at least two trips to break up the season so I will definitely take you up on that offer, if not sooner."

Ignacio places his hand over mine and gently squeezes.

After fueling up on java, we lazily drift on Angell Street back to downtown. Amiga's tongue wags the whole way.

The three of us pass by Memorial Boulevard as we did when we first arrived. We snap some selfies along the river with the mall towering in the background. I post one of the three of us on my Instagram with the hashtag: summer days.

When we reach the state house, we race to the top of the steps. And once there under the grand white columns, we take some more photos. Ignacio leans over and kisses me on the lips.

"I had a great day here, Tommy. Thank you."

I kiss him back on the lips.

From our perch, we stand shoulder to shoulder, taking in the amazing view of the mall, the grid-like downtown, the hilly slopes of Brown. The fleeting rays of sunlight cast a pinkish glow over the city.

We hold hands and descend the steps back to the car. As Ignacio and Amiga climb inside, I stand outside the Beetle, my right elbow leaning on the car's roof. I look around and study the view once more.

I take a deep breath and exhale. I grin.

I drive the VW out of Providence and hop on the green ramp north toward Interstate 95, passing the behemoth mall on the right. As I drive, Ignacio's left fingers entwine with mine.

When I glance in the rear view mirror, I notice that Amiga is sound asleep, probably worn out from all the walking. I whoosh by the statehouse and Providence increasingly recedes in the rear view mirror.

Ignacio and I don't talk much during the drive. Instead, we smile at one another and listen to some light pop music. We hold hands and enjoy the trip home.

Half an hour into the drive, we approach the sign for Foxboro, Ignacio passes out. He sleeps on his side, his face toward the window. I softly caress the back of his head. And silently, I mouth, I love you.

23

IT'S FINALLY MY turn down the aisle. For once, I'm not the person writing about the wedding. I'm living it. And for once, I'm the groom. Not the best man or the one who gives the toast. Those duties have been relegated to my best buds, Rico and Carlos who are helping me get ready at the inn. Danny is here and hovering all around us to capture the behind-the-scenes moments with his camera.

"Loco, you look so handsome. See, I knew your time would come, " Carlos says. He's standing before me by the mirror and adjusting my red necktie. It's the same one that the boutique owner gave me for the photo shoot from a few months ago.

"Thanks Carlos. This is surreal. I can't believe this is happening!"

"It's happening, silly goose! But I knew you'd make a guy semi-sort of happy some day and you found him in Mr. Panama!" Rico teases, standing behind me as he straightens the back of my grey suit.

"Um, Costa Rica, Rico!" I chide him, giving him a sideways smirk.

"Yeah, yeah, same thing," he says with a mischievous wink as he then makes room for himself in front of the mirror.

"You know I'm only fucking with you! Anything to make you a little more nervous."

"I'm not nervous!" I declare.

"YEAH, RIGHT!" the guys shout at the same time.

"You have a little bit of sweat on your upper lip. Dab it with your red handkerchief or else it's going to come out in these photos. Hey, the wedding music is just beginning to play. That's our cue. It's now or never. Tommy, are you ready, GROOM MAN! I can't call you BEST MAN, anymore," Danny says.

He holds up his camera above us as we huddle to take a group selfie.

"Everyone say BOSTON BOYS ON TOP!" Danny instructs.

We shout it like a cheerleading squad. His camera goes *click click click*.

I give myself one more review in the mirror. I flash a thumbs up. Then I swallow a big gulp of air. With each hand, I grab one of Rico and Carlos's hands. I look at both of them and smile. And they smile back. Danny stands before us once again. He shoots some more photos as we prepare to leave the room at the inn and head outside to the garden.

"I'm ready!" I tell them with a tremulous smile.

Six months ago, I didn't see this coming. I don't think Ignacio did either or maybe he did. I was ready to wish him a fond farewell to Fort Lauderdale. I accepted that he would be starting a new life in the tropics while I continued mine in Maine. But then life threw me one of those Boston Red sox curveballs. Instead of running from it, I caught it. Let me explain.

I did say goodbye to Ignacio. During our last night together, I surprised him with a dinner at my place. (I didn't cook it. I ordered some Thai food and a bottle of champagne in case you were wondering.)

After dinner, we made a toast with our glasses.

"Here's to you and Amiga and to your new life!" I held up my glass and clinked it to Ignacio's.

"I...love...you, Tommy," Ignacio said his voice filled with emotion. We had settled on my sofa where our legs entwined. My left hand caressed his right hand.

As he looked at me longingly, I took a deep breath and smiled. I finally said those magical three words out loud to him. "I love you!"

It felt so good to release those words and share them with his caring, handsome man who captured my heart.

I was in love and I liked the way it sounded and felt - like pure happiness floating through my veins.

Ignacio's eyes widened and glistened. He then moved closer and kissed me softly.

"I knew you did. I sensed it. I just wanted you to say it when you were ready. It had to come from your heart. I'm going to miss you so much. Hopefully you'll visit soon," he whispered into my ear. His stubble tickled my cheek and earlobe.

"I promise I'll do my best to come down as soon as I can, Ignacio. Besides, I think I need to get my color back," I said, extending my pale slightly hairy arms.

Ignacio grinned.

"I love your arms just the way they are, Tommy. Don't change anything about you, guapo."

He left the Sunday before Labor Day. Although Ignacio wasn't physically in Maine, he was still with me in other ways. We texted or Skyped every day. He held up Amiga on camera so I could say Hi. She playfully barked when she saw me appear on his laptop's screen.

Each day, I looked forward to these chats. I shared with him my latest interview. Ignacio talked about his day at the hotel in Fort Lauderdale. It didn't matter what we talked about. We were communicating, bonding.

To my surprise, the relationship endured and blossomed from 1,600 miles away.

Each day, my heart ached for him. Those messages and communications only endeared me more to him. I didn't feel so alone anymore in Ogunquit. In fact, I felt the opposite.

After a month, I couldn't wait to see him, kiss him any longer. So I booked a flight from Boston to Fort Lauderdale for a long weekend.

As soon as I emerged from the terminal, Ignacio and Amiga greeted me. The kiss Ignacio and I shared was more potent than our first, like fireworks blazing across the night sky. And after that weekend in Fort Lauderdale, I knew I didn't want to be apart from him for so long, or ever again. I knew for certain that in Ignacio, I had found my partner. And with him and Amiga, I had a new little family.

"Maybe you can move down here at some point?" he suggested as we lounged in his bed one morning that weekend. The sun slanted through his blinds and highlighted his hazel eyes and his trimmed chest hair.

"If I found the right job. The local papers probably couldn't match my *People* salary. In the meantime, I'll start looking and see what's out there. It won't hurt to look."

"Or you can move back up to Maine," I countered.

To that idea, Ignacio twisted his nose and shook his head side to side.

"Only during the spring and summer!" Ignacio declared with a grin.

"Well, we'll figure something out, Ignacio."

"As long as we're together, guapo," he said.

And Amiga barked to get the last word in, of course.

I flew back and forth between Fort Lauderdale and Boston for the next few months. I didn't mind the warmer weather as Maine morphed into its frozen tundra state. Ignacio managed to visit me once in Ogunquit during winter. It happened to be a blistery January weekend when about six inches of snow fell over the area. Temperatures hovered around 30-degrees. I had to scrape snow off the windshield of my Volkswagen and salt the walkway outside my front door.

Ignacio was content staying inside with Amiga because there wasn't much to do outside. Ogunquit transformed into the seasonal ghost town once again, something out of *The Walking Dead* sans the zombies. The snow wasn't agreeing with him or Amiga.

"I think we've seen enough snow for a while," he said as I drove him back to Logan for his flight to South Florida. Amiga trembled in the back seat.

"It wasn't that bad, Ignacio," I turned to him.

"I'm a frozen Costa Rican! It will take the whole flight for me to thaw out. Right, Amiga?" he said, looking down at the dog who easily blended in with the snow outside my window.

And like snow, a solution to our long-distance relationship seemed to fall out of the sky.

My magazine posted a new job opening for a correspondent to cover the southeastern United States and the Caribbean as coverage warranted. The person would be based out of Miami or Atlanta, depending on where he or she preferred to live. Similar in description to my current position, the job called for regional travel to report on stories of interest from breaking news to celebrity features. When the corporate email popped into my inbox in January, I smiled. Maybe this was the way for Ignacio and I to be together – in the same state.

Don't get me wrong. It's not that I grew tired of living in New England. I loved my home. Boston and Ogunquit had been great to me over the years. They afforded me a good career and lifelong friendships. But another new home awaited. I felt this was my chance to embark on that journey. I applied for the job. And three weeks later in February, my editors informed me that I would be relocating south. I thanked them profusely and told them that I would like to be based in Fort Lauderdale which was close enough to Miami, my hometown. A life with Ignacio began to align.

While Rico and Carlos were sad to see me leave New England, they also knew that I would visit and they each would have a place to stay in South Florida.

"Go be with your man, loco!" Carlos said when I called him with the news.

"Besides, Nick and I visit my dad down there so we'll definitely be seeing you in Miami. I'm not going to lie. It's not going to be the same as having you an hour away from me but if this is what you want, then go for it, loco. You have my support."

Rico was more dramatic and direct.

"What will you do without your wingman to fucking guide you?" he said when I called him after Carlos with the news.

"Don't you mean what will you do without me?" I teased.

"I'm really happy for you, buddy. I suspected that one day, you might move back home. Now we'll truly be wingmen, flying back and forth to hang out. I love you, silly goose!"

"I love you too, old friend!"

"Wait, who are you calling old?" Rico said.

Ignacio proposed to me on my first night in Fort Lauderdale. I didn't see the proposal coming. Amiga conspired with him. When I arrived at our apartment (yes, we moved in together), there was a bouquet of roses waiting for me on the dining table. As I sniffed the flowers, Amiga darted up to me with a red box tied around her collar.

Her tail thumped happily. When I bent down to take a closer look, the box had my name scrawled on it. When I opened it, there was a shiny ring with a note attached that read, "Will you marry us, Tommy Perez?"

Then Ignacio got down on bended knee next to Amiga. How could I say no to this adorable scene!

And so here I am on this lovely sunny spring day, slowly walking out of the inn's hallway and toward the back garden that faces the infamous cliff walk in lovely Ogunquit. A cool gentle breeze greets me as I take the first few steps toward a new life with Ignacio. We decided to marry where we first met. Ogunquit will always hold a special place in my heart and Ignacio's.

It's a small ceremony of about 10 people on the lawn of the inn where Ignacio used to work. The gardens burst with tulips and pansies, all various shades of the color spectrum. Ignacio's immediate family - his younger brother, sister, her husband and two children - flew up for the nuptials. They're seated on white chairs that take up two rows that face the ocean. Cool breezes blow in and carry the smell of fresh mulch from the garden.

My guests are a mix of friends and ...wait! Is that Kyle sitting behind Rico's husband and fanning himself with a napkin? Wearing a pair of oversized Jackie O' sunglasses, Kyle flamboyantly waves to me as I step onto the garden. Shouldn't he be auditioning for a new reality show or something? Oh well. As long as he doesn't make a scene, he's welcome to stay.

My sister and my father didn't come to the wedding. He's 85 and his issues with walking long distances make travel difficult so he stayed in Miami with my sister but I know they're here in spirit.

As an instrumental version of Elton John's *Circle of Life* softly plays from the inn's speakers, Amiga in her custom made white doggie dress waddles down the aisle before jumping onto the lap of Ignacio's sister. We wanted to include Amiga in the festivities because, well, why not? Then my best men, Carlos, followed by Rico walk down the aisle.

They take their positions to the right of the podium where Dr. Bella Solis stands gracefully while holding a book of proverbs. (She offered to officiate the ceremony.) And standing next to her is Ignacio wearing a charcoal grey suit with a red necktie that matches mine.

With his hands folded in front of his jacket, he winks at me as if to say "You got this guapo!"

I grin back.

A small purple and yellow butterfly flutters all around me as I slowly glide past the rows of our lovely guests who include Dr. Bella's son Elias and his boyfriend Otto from Germany. I'd like to think that the butterfly is my mom escorting me on this important day since purple was her favorite color.

Speaking of butterflies, my tummy is filled with them, big and small as they dart all around my rib cage. Tears begin to form in my eyes making everything look slightly underwater. I blink back the tears and focus. I'm feeling a swirl of emotions from happy and proud to nervous and fear. To calm my nerves, I finger my red necktie to make sure that it's still there and for good luck.

But I don't think I'll be needing luck today. Standing next to Ignacio is Rico, Carlos and Danny with his camera, my Boston Boys Club. As I walk toward my new life, I have everything that I ever wanted right here in front of me.

Who's Johnny?

 Johnny Diaz is a features reporter at the South Florida Sun Sentinel. Prior to that, he was a media writer for The Boston Globe's Business section, where he covered TV news, radio, print and advertising. Johnny was also a features writer for The Globe's Living/Arts section for three years. Before that he was a general assignment Metro reporter for his hometown newspaper, The Miami Herald. Johnny is the author of *Boston Boys Club, Miami Manhunt, Beantown Cubans* and *Take the Lead* and *Looking for Providence*. The Spanish version of *Take the Lead* is *Tomar La Iniciativa*. Johnny lives in Miami, Florida. Readers can visit his website: ***www.beantowncuban.com***

Made in the USA
Columbia, SC
26 March 2019